Tony

Dada

Co Loa Media

Dada

Tony Wailey was born in Liverpool in 1947. He worked as a seafarer and construction worker for ten years. He later studied modern history and wrote a thesis on the Liverpool Seamen. For a quarter of a century he was an advisor to mature students in Universities and Colleges of adult education. He now works as a freelance writer. This is his fifth novel.

Dada

Tony Wailey

Co Loa Media

First published 2020 by Co Loa Media

Co Loa Media
Cheltenham
GLOS
GL52 2DA

ISBN: 978 0 9928962 8 7

Designed and typeset by iKraal, Cape Town SA
Printed and bound by CPI Group (UK) Ltd, Croydon, CR0 4YY

For Simon Edwards

'Don't beat him,' the judge, Malay, says.

They depart as they have come, in whispers. I resume my thoughts of Mo. He has not written apart from that one cursory letter that attempts to explain his actions at the trial.

'We are criminals before the law and even before your final act,' he wrote.

He does not want to be associated, either by sex or deed with a condemned man. He might be ill or dead now, slaughtered by my friends Iskra and Shabela. They might have found his betrayal too much to bear in the heat and nervous stench of the court room. He tells me he has to speak the truth and truth will always live. How can I know anything about that? Apart from our bodies there is nothing to remind us of each other. His fear of being caught and labelled is greater than his love for me, me, the most damaged or disengaged in the first place makes it all the more ironic. Maybe this is part of the illusion where nothing seems as it is and nothing is about what it's really about.

Suppose Mo is dead. His memory would move to another place. We always regard the dead with more affection than the living. I suppose that's quite right. Their time has gone. There is nothing more to say, no more wriggling or turning with this messy business of life. I could not feign an interest. This seems to me quite normal. People would soon forget me when I'd been hung by the neck. Even this is not too hard to stomach. There is no idea in this world that you can't get used to in time, not even the fact of your own oblivion.

My thoughts reach this point when suddenly the door swings open and the chief of the holy ones appears. He has opened my cell with his own key and without guards or judge. He approaches me directly. He awakens me from my reverie. I give a jump. He tells me not to worry; it's natural for a man in my condition. I remind him again that his presence is only required when they come to walk me to the gallows. What is he doing here if it isn't for that time? I notice the beads in his hand and give out a groan.

'This is just a friendly visit,' he says.

It has no bearing on any outcome of my appeal. He sits down on my bed and asks me to raise myself and sit behind him. I refuse and he looks hurt. He has a soft kindly face and I feel bad ignoring him but then I think, fuck him. He's the one imposing on me.

He remains quite still at first, his arms resting on his knees, his eyes fixed upon his hands, as if in repentance. They are gnarled but sinewy and look like they have spent time in the jungle or the garden. He gently rubs them together and lays them on his face as if gathering energy for the task ahead. The beads clack. I can picture him tending his flowers and vegetables much like my Dada tended on the balcony or his allotment at the old people's home. My father hates the intimate name Dada has given himself for me, just as Dada can't stand my mother's husband, who is Malay and wants everybody to behave correctly. Maybe there is a black hut on the borders of the holy man's path like the one Dada keeps for his drinking. He stays so long in this position and I'm so busy imagining all the parts of his garden that I quite forget he is there.

Suddenly he springs up and I hear the beads dance. He looks down upon me.

'Why' he asks 'won't you let me refresh you?'

'Because I don't need you' I say.

'Are you really so sure of that' he says.

I tell him about my surge of freedom, the unpicking of the noose and the process of my appeal.

'They are the things that concern me' I say, 'whether I believe you is not the point.'

'I cannot answer that' he says.

He looks away and without altering his posture asks if it is because I am utterly desperate that I should act like this? I answer him no. I am scared enough, that's true but who wouldn't be in my position?

'In that case' he says 'God/ Allah/The Almighty Buddha can help you. All the ones I have seen in your position have turned to them in their time of trouble.'

'They are at liberty to do so' I answer him. If they want to be helped then let God help them but I have no time to work up any interest in things that do not concern me.

He flutters his hands. Drawing himself up, he smooths his clothes, just like the detective with his Chinese eyes when he gave me the once over in that brown office that seems so long ago. It's not because I have been condemned, he says, that he speaks to me in such a personal way. In his opinion every person on earth is under sentence of death.

'Is that the same thing?' I ask. 'It's the same as saying no-one can say anything because they do not have all the facts. It provides no consolation. What would my gangster friend Iskra think of that? What will he do with another forty years of venturing out each morning to greet the outcomes of his own dirty work, laugh that is what he'll do?'

The holy man says, 'We will all die and if your death comes sooner we still have to face the same truth.

How will you face that terrible hour?'

He turns to me quickly and gazes into my eyes.

I'm supposed to look away, discomforted. He has obviously done this many times before. It doesn't wash with me. I have played that game every morning at the dock or when the old ladies come with their shawls or summer wraps to bargain for cheap fish or the crowds on Sunday hope to beat me down. It's the same as those who have died on the Thai fishing boats that night because of the quiet way they bring the Burmese women ashore, around the back of the dock, the only time they show them respect, then you know. That is the real bargain. All the rest is make believe. The old think they are the best at it and very few can change the young in the matter of who they think they are but it is only chance that includes me. That is what the holy man wants off me, a bargain, something for free. But I'd been around this block many times with Mo and old Srino who lives in our building and they always blink and look away first, even Iskra. I hear the beads rattle again and know what is coming.

The holy one's voice is steady.

'Have you no hope at all' he asks. 'Do you really think that when you die nothing remains?'

'Yes,' I say.

He drops his eyes and sits down. He's truly sorry for me he says. Life must be unbearable for a man to think in such a manner, for the end to mean surely the end.

I shrug and look away.

It is no different than the time in that hot little room with the detective and the Malay clerk typing behind my shoulder with his sad onion breath or the prosecutor when he sits down on his folded robes, his eyes roll like stones towards me, and he calls for the maximum sentence.

I begin to get bored. I try to pull off my usual trick; to nod and go silent in the event of him leaving me alone. It's an old Sea Dayak move. My people are the first to bend and the last to break. They are here in Borneo before all the Sultans, Rajahs and Tuns arrive with blood on their hands, a resistance to oppression by saying nothing. I even catch the ochre smell of the office walls from that other time.

'Your appeal has not succeeded,' the holy man says.

I do not bother to answer. Why show him my thoughts? I think of the executioner's knot and how they will tighten it. He is questioning me again. I have not showed enough repentance. His voice rises slightly and he seems distressed. He says that even if my appeal had succeeded I still carry a huge burden of guilt. It is riddled through me like a cancer is his expression; guilt enough to cause any death of the soul he says.

'Man's justice is a vain thing, only God's justice matters', he says.

I point out that I had been condemned by man's justice. He agrees but he says that alone would not clear the stain of my sin before God. I tell him I am not conscious of any sin. All I know is that I have been found guilty of a criminal offence and whether premeditated or not it is not my way of looking at things. I am to die for that crime; no matter how much chance has played in the course of events that day.

'You are mistaken' he says. His voice is grave. 'More is required of you than you are prepared to give or may be asked. I have looked at photographs of those poor boys …,' he breaks off.

'In the matter of human stain' I say, 'I am not an expert.'
'What chance did you give them?' He looks away.
'These walls are steeped in human suffering. It always makes me shudder at what has been contained within them. The deepest nature of a man's heart lies here. And yet within the depths of this profanity, there sometimes comes a single light with the worst darkness like a lamp cast upon the sea.'
'Does a man's life end with the lighting of a lamp?' I ask. 'I have been standing at these walls for months. You are right, there do come pictures and images and memories and arousals but never a single light. Once upon a time I used to search for it and perhaps a face, but it is always a face from the beach or eyes that glow with desire for me, such as Mo's. I have never seen any light or form that guides me amidst the grey bitumen of these bricks.'
He asks if he might touch my hand in a final farewell.
'No' I say. 'I have had enough of touching.'
He slowly draws his hand along the wall so as his fingers leave traces along the block as if the light that resides there had once sketched across all these islands of this archipelago they call the Greater Sunda.
'Do you really love these earthly things so much' he asks.
I do not answer him. All of sudden he explodes in a way much stronger than the early interviews with the detective for he is a quieter and more contained man than the police officer and his paroxysms appear all the greater. His face puffs up and the eyes grow bright in their dark hoods.
'No, No, No I refuse to believe it. Do you not see there is a life that comes after us and is there before us for

those who prepare? The sloughing away of the human body is nothing but preparation for the spirit to come.'

'Of course,' I say. 'Everyone has that wish at times but that it's just the same as wanting to be rich or to swim very fast or to catch the best looker at a dance,' I think of Mo again.

Maybe the way he looks then, sad, contrite, even upset, I feel a bit sorry for him. What is about to break inside me also becomes suddenly quiet. The insults about to be unleashed, the useless blasphemous prayers I keep from shouting, to burn rather than to disappear, all this is locked within me, the ecstasy and joy and rage bursting inside but I remain quiet. I make no sound as if all of his pieties are worth no more than one afternoon in the sun. I would not have cared who comes to the room then, even the executioner himself; I would have taken him into my arms as I first kissed Mo in the picture house, below the gaze of this unholy State.

The holy man holds to his own but to me he is death. If my hands are empty now and my fate assured, his hopes and wishes have not done me down. I have seized life, seized the time around me; not intended for me but that has happened anyway. I act and it has not been otherwise. What is done is done and I face my own bridge of anxiety. What does it mean? Maybe since Dada's funeral and the extinguishing of his own holy flame I have been waiting for this, waiting for the moment to rise before me like a pirate within a storm, any hopes of safe harbour gone yet battling still the wind.

'Who is this man you call Dada?' he asks.

'My grandfather,' I say.

'Then let us talk about him,' he says.

'No' I say, 'Let's discuss my father.'

'I remember when he returns to the room from his sojourn to the outhouse with the young Kalimantan. My mother starts to get up from her chair to go through to the kitchen. She always does that. I lay my hand gently on her shoulder.

'Not this time ma' I say.

'My father reaches to his waist. A bead of sweat drips from his moustache. His white shirt is lightly stained from the food we had eaten that evening. Rain starts to hammer against the blinds. At first you can hear the tack tack tack against the windows and then the rivers streaming down the panes and the lightning crackle in the trees.

'"Your Dada could have ruined the very foundation of this island and all the Kampongs of the peninsula with his communism. Do you know the circumstances of his birth?" My father's belt is out now and raised.

'I pick up a knife from the kitchen work top and hold it, the steel jutting from my fingers the way our pirates hold the *Kris*.

'"Come near me and I will put this" I raise the blade "just below your ribs."

'My mother screams. I ask her to keep quiet, please be quiet.'

'And then?' the holy man asks.

'He tells me the secret. The secret of my Dada's birth; I put the knife down and leave home, leave my studies and go and live on the dock,' I say

'And does it help you,' he asks.

'It goes with my identity,' I reply.

Maybe the holy man is trying to connect me with my

history but, nothing, nothing, can shift the importance of that night, nor others where I safely navigate from sailing around the earth from a beautiful amphetamine journey, lost amongst the stars until that moment the universe comes to shatter all around me with the wind that runs with the rain and the sun to the fish dock where I work and from there to this cell and to this very moment, a spirit that blows through my whole life.

The holy man looks at me. He can leave now. He understands my sudden spurts and pauses, my silences, my need for everything to be quiet. On his way, he levels all the ideals and duress people have tried to foist on me during those long years of my journey beneath the arc of my father's fear.

Who are the 'White Rajahs' themselves if not pirates dressed in their tropical linens and silks and what difference can the little woman dressed all in blue make to me with her infantile stories and their hold upon our family?

'Behind every great fortune is a great crime,' she says.

'And who is this woman?' the holy man asks.

I shake my head. What difference can any oracle make to me now? The 'Malayness' of my parents and their disobedient, disoriented child on his way to the gallows and my half Dayak, half White, Chinese Dada who is trapped, ignored and butchered in their thoughts.

'I can see you are confused,' the holy man says.

Thoughts harden into habits. Institutions of blood and matter become fixed totems instead of being scattered in freedom across the sea, words jumble and dance in my head, the Dada's love, the holy one's words, the gentleness of Mo and a crime of murder all go against me in all these stolen moments. Whatever way you look at it, the way you choose to live has nothing to do with justice.

'He used to shout from a balcony full of flowers,' I say. Tears brim in my eyes.

'You who are so far away from us have been brought close. We are the peace between you, between Chinese, Malay and Dayak. The union makes us peacemakers and breaks all barriers they use to keep us apart here; broken by hostility, caused by rulers, decreed by shipping laws from across the sea, they bind us to the frontiers of this island. The frontier of their own repression is where the Queen sits with her brigands, colonisers and rajahs in the great empire city. Our union unites us in peace. Peace to you who are so far away and peace to those who come near us; its spirit guides us all.'

'You do not choose fate, it chooses you.' I say to him. 'The same way time runs through you. We do not live through time, it is not ours.'

The holy man shifts uncomfortably on the bench.

'Can you not see that every man or women is privileged, not just the castes or the races, the "aks", the "ans" and the "ese" of this windblown island,' I say.

'There is only one class of human, the privileged class, those lucky to be alive,' he replies.

I ask him if they include the outsiders and the quiet, the drug users and those who sojourn, all with the gift of life, all condemned to die.

He shakes his head. He is quite right about this. What difference would it make if his execution takes place instead of my own? Would he not weep the same tears as me?

It is all the same in the end. What does it matter if

at this very moment Mo is kissing his new boyfriend and eating lamb's kidneys? Would he be executed as a sodomite in accordance with the laws of this land or lauded as prosecution witness in mitigation for his crime. As a condemned man himself can he not see, nor feel that dark wind blowing or remember the smell of his lover's Cologne?

'God bless you,' the holy man says. He tries to close the door quietly behind him.

When I hear the lock clack back into its ratchet, I release my breath, and shout, bellow and scream at the walls. The guards come running but they know better than to approach me. I hurl the chair and metal basin, break the wood upon the bed, and try to fire the mattress. I know nothing of my strength in such a vortex. Then I look and see a moon and a night I can imagine scented with flowers and I rebel again in screams and anger at such abundance.

The commotion unsettles me but by the time it reaches its final ebb, I lie upon the floor and sleep well. A long sleep for me but the stars are still out in the sky and I can imagine the sound of the city and the river and beyond it and all the smells of the country. The marvellous peace of a summer's night floods through me. Just on daybreak I hear the throb of a trawler's engines coming close to the dock and think of the women below deck, carried in bundles to the wharf with the drugs hidden in carpets and baskets of fish.

People are starting on a voyage that no longer concerns me. Dada feels close to me now. I understand his life with his ships, lovers and friends and how he has to live with his actions.

Going to that Home is just an extension to the life he

has lived for years here in the city with his stories, his laughter and songs of Liverpool and the Blue Funnel Line. In the Home there is no escape from them with Kim Song his old shipmate. I suppose he must have been happy where lives are flickering and tapering all around him like candles. It is always important to remember as many stories as possible as it is important to forget the other stuff. 'Dada', my father hates that word.

Blasphemous they call him but they do not refuse his money. With death so near, he must have felt on the brink of freedom. He has lived under so many rulers, the English, the Chinese, the Japanese and Malays, despised and hated by them all. He can see through them like a glass window and still laugh. He can see the gauze and artifice design of the culture they build to protect themselves. What is taken from the pirates is avoided in the way they practice the truth. No one has any right to weep for him.

I am ready to start again; the great gash of anger has cleaned me of hope, hope of the unravelling rope and any appeal of sentence. I am ready now to stare at the sky with its stars and patterns and the brilliant light radiating from the moon, I feel my heart open to the great silence. To feel myself as part of its huge indifference; its washing of history and time like lightning amongst the trees of the village where the Dada can clearly see me, my blood, my line.

I understand that I have once been happy and that I would be happy again. All that is needed now is for the crowds to show, festooned crowds in flowered shirts that would billow around the prison walls on the day of my execution. To call for my obliteration and to cheer at the hour of its coming and none more so than the Kalimantans spread across this great western island of Indonesia.

And there would be crowds. They shoot the guilty across the border. The police have to clear the roads, the way thousands turn up all bright in all their colours to raise an almighty cheer when the rifles go off and the smell of wood smoke rises in the air. Would I remind them in their celebrations of the times I had made love to Mo and brought all the laws of this usurped place crashing down upon my head as a sodomite and a murderer.

When they drop me through the trap, I'll take the pain and my spirits will also dance in strange celebration. They will press and clamour inside my skull and I will embrace the great blaze of light. When news of my death shall reach the outside all I can hope is that they raise the same cheers for me, Rana Abdullah, the pirate.

Dada will certainly do so from the grave, the grandson of the last white Rajah; the child who is father to the man. I shall need no hood. I want them to see my eyes bulge and my neck snap and to accompany my fall into universal darkness with song.

The time that is left suddenly shines clear before me. I hope the news will spread like wildfire to all the districts, diocese and kampongs of this sceptre of an island; Borneo a paradise that lives like a hell, a hell disguised as paradise, a corrupted, broken howl of different tongues since Magellan's fleet first landed here and witnessed its sparkling rivers and rocky green harbours.

Chapter Two

A lady in blue

No more holy men. I have nothing to say to them. I don't feel like talking. I shall see them soon anyhow. They'll all be snivelling around the gallows after I'm gone. They don't do executions in public any more. The only thing that interests me now is the issue of getting around the procedures to see if there is a loophole in all that tight moral armoury of their precious law. They have moved me to a different cell. Is that Iskra's work? It's more comfortable in this one, lying on my back; I can see more than a portion of the sky. Maybe that is the reason they move you here. To give you those last looks at what you are going to lose. Seeing the soft underbelly of the clouds sending the city pink and black in the last of the sunset is worth a lot to a condemned man. There is nothing much else to see but I can construct a whole world in those clutches of clouds. All my time is spent in watching the slowly moving colours of the day and even of the night. It always surprises you if you gaze and wait. Night also has its own colour. I do not care when I sleep or wake.

My friend Shabela ends every sentence by saying, 'and with the blessing of God.' I laugh at myself to hear it now.

The problem of a loophole obsesses me. I am always wondering if there have been cases of condemned prisoners escaping from the implacable machinery of justice. At the last moment they break through the police cordon and vanish to the jungle in a nick of time, just before the noose is uncoiled. There would have been more chance if they held the hangings in public like they used to. I blame myself now for not paying attention. I used to read about them in the history books or scattered papers; of prisoners jumping the scaffold and being shot as they ran away. That would be something. When you are on the move there is always a chance. It is like a thief running down the dockside with a basket of fish, running for his life, looking ahead but waiting for the shot to gouge open his back; all of his life contained in that one moment, everything before him.

You should always take account of such matters. I let them go missing. I suppose that if something doesn't concern you, you don't bother. I'd read descriptions of hangings but they haven't stayed with me long, but now facing my own, it is surprising what the mind stores. What it brings together between your own circumstances and what is before you. Technical books that show the placing of the knot certainly exist but I have never felt interested enough to look them up. If they are dealing with pirates or hanging them on a ship, of huge lashings, keel haulings or walking the gangplank in chains, that would be more interesting.

There is always the chance of jumping or going adrift. This appeals to me.

'Hanging is the white man's way, the civilised way;' Iskra once said to me.

'Even the hood they use puts you at a distance. They don't want to see your eyes.'

They don't like to see the face of the condemned man but these executioners will certainly see me. Surely there must be cases when the rope has slipped or the drop is blocked or that chance or luck plays a happy part. It's easy to think of the pirates and my own heritage, one who rides and steals these waters and laughs at any mishap. Within the normal processes of justice it would do me. My emotions would take care of the rest, shredding their law like leaves.

The papers often talk of a debt to society and payment to the one offended. But that sort of talk doesn't fire the imagination. No, the thing that counts is to make a dash for it, to defeat the rules, make a mad stampede to freedom along the docks and quays and dive to the water, shark ridden or not; a gambler's last throw. Naturally if other pirates caught you then watch out but at least there is always the chance. Kill or be killed rather than this slow and brutal wheel of justice.

The process is as sad as Old Srino and his missing bird. Srino lives in a room in our building with his parrot. He hates it and as far as you can tell the parrot hates him. They are both scaly with age and wear just like any old couple that get to resemble each other.

One day the bird goes missing; hops out of its cage at the fairground and sets itself free. It could hardly walk let alone fly. The sun would kill it before other birds. Does it just want away from Srino and the madness of life around him or is it a genuine bid for freedom? Either way he is devastated. I draw on my wooden chip of a cigarette and think maybe the bird just took a chance. Shrino always opens the cage for him either as threat or temptation and the bird must have thought, 'This is my chance old man.'

Since the loss he always appears at my doorway at night. Thinking of his bird distracts me from my own situation. They can deprive you of sex and cigarettes in here but not of time to think.

'Time on the anchor is time on the nail,' Dada used to say.

It's a curious world between being neither here nor there in prison, not at sea or in port. When a ship's engines stop beating it loses its soul or when someone like me stops running.

But they can't deprive me of his song. I remember him shouting from his balcony and the constant visits from the police.

'Brothers and sisters' Dada would sing, 'our time grows short and those who own the ships owe us much. Those who have wives should live as though they had none. Those who mourn for our impending loss should live as if they had nothing to mourn; those full of abundance that are enjoying life should live as though there was nothing to laugh about. For truly now, we have only ourselves to offer but only when we have *our* freedom; a demand from neither Dayak, Malay nor Chinese but for all seamen of this island.'

His voice sings this out in an odd, sort of ringing fairground voice. Some would laugh, most of them immigrants from over the border; maybe that's why the Malays hate him and called him traitor.

His song comes from the birth of this nation more than fifty years ago. Time is of no matter to him, he sings until he goes up river to the old people's home and even then it does not stop him.

Try as I might I could not picture myself hanging from a scaffold in some quiet room reserved by the State for the condemned, my hands tied behind me. When you think about it there is always a distortion on how they base their judgement and the sequence of events that run up to it. Before they deliver their verdict there is no intention on my part to kill a soul. I find myself manipulated; in the middle of something outside my being and twisted like a small wooden doll. History washes me along its broken path as if a bottle suddenly dances on the tide; fate more than premeditation; chance rather than deliberation is the cause of my case.

'Don't forget I know you inside out,' the woman in blue says.

The fact that they give the verdict so late in the afternoon when it might have been done just after lunch, when the balance of the sky turns different, the clouds softer, the possibility of sun; all of this would made it better , more palatable, easier for a person like me, who cries each morning with joy and thanks.

At some point of the day we are all naked. Why make such a fuss of our great nation stuff when everyone knows we hate each other here, Chinese, Malay, Malaneu or Dayak. We just have to rub along, get on with our own lives. All of this cultural stuff surrounds us like a clogged drain. It deprives us of certainty.

I remember reading once in the night of a murderer in southern Italy. Naples I think somewhere certainly in the south, where they used to grant a last request outside the jail wall. This prisoner asks for a leg of lamb, a bottle of grappa and a young woman. He pays for it all via his family. The authorities make sure they bring his bag of gold coin to the prison. When the time comes for his death his hair has turned white and stands upright above his haggard face. This is the only way to lose a life, to lose it with desperation, despair and longing. Everything else is a lie. Those who say different are ones who have never experienced the decision.

On the Peninsula my father once attends an execution when they were performed in public. He returns home full of righteousness. He tells my mother justice has been done. She asks him to describe it to her in detail and when he does so, she takes a shivering fit. She is soft and tender at heart my mother but she is badly influenced by him. She has to have a blanket brought to her. Maybe in the open is the only way you can genuinely interest anyone in the taking of a life. If I ever get out of this mess I will attend every execution in my lifetime. It is the only way to tell if you are truly alive. My father never fails to omit that this is the punishment given to all who pretend to be what they are not. Anyone who goes against the State in his books is a traitor and in the pay of foreigners or communists. He gives me an uncertain look before the beatings begin again.

From the moment they give the verdict, my results are clear. All the rest of the machinery and laws of the Federation now swing into action, as tangible as the wall against which I lie and utterly indifferent to the pale movement of the sky above me.

Unwise to even consider a possibility of release, for just one moment I picture myself in freedom, standing beside a double rank of policemen outside the prison walls, an onlooker who has come to attend the final show, who could go home afterwards and be free to do his drugs in a quiet meditative state. The thought floods my mind with a wild exultation like the wind that blows down from the great mountain of Kinabalu to the north. The weaving, tattooing and log houses of our Dayak traditional industries are long gone in the face of satellite TV and our sweet medicine from Thailand. It is stupid to let my imagination run away with me like this. A moment later and I am shivering myself and wrap myself in a sheet. Even my mouth seems to tremble.

Another of my fancies is to make up new laws that clearly state that when you mean to do something – only then can you be punished. If you had no prior thoughts, you could not be found guilty. Your crime has to be pure premeditated. It gives more of a chance that way, even if it's only a dog's chance. They would soon clear that up but as rule there should be a slip in the knot, one time out of a thousand that gives anyone like me a slim hope of release, like the amnesty for a President's birthday, a Sultan's anniversary or a Dictator's revolution. Materials such as the rope, the garrotte or the guillotine give nothing back except the certainty of a death ordained.

Death indeed; I don't know about the rope. They would just start again if the knot slipped. But say the knot kept on slipping? Would they call this 'an act of god' and let you live? Would you feel the spirits pour back into those areas they strangle; the pain of the blood channels squeezed tight then fill up again with oxygen? The pain might torment you but at least you would still be here.

Every condemned man needs to have this hope in his

system otherwise, what is the point. They could take you out in the yard and shoot you on the stones and let your parents pay for the bullet like they do in China. If it comes to this, the condemned have to collaborate with the system of the accusers so everything could all pass off without a hitch. But this is a tricky business. *Things might get out of hand* is the unspoken thought. In return for collaboration, the prisoner is 'given' respect. Bring me to the table of Russian roulette any day, with two gulps of freedom between each bullet and more precious, my time beneath the sky between court room and prison.

But wait, if all is pre-ordained, who would let you imagine a different way of reckoning? One of our teachers used to talk of 'the instant second' of literature as a mirror, that if you wanted to 'see' one place in your mind, you thought about another. What would my thoughts show? I got to thinking about hangings I'd heard of in the past, of pirates hanging from gallows at the movies while the crowd below gaze and cheer and watch them swing. Not just at the movies but when the white rajahs came to this island and strung up the rebels; did my great grandmother scream before or after they raped her? What is that second like when the knot quickens and your feet dangle?

Does it last a lifetime after they stretch the hood over you? Does everything grow bright before the rope jumps, the trap opens and your neck snaps? Is it the same if they kill you privately, discreetly, behind a prison wall with a hint of shame and a great deal of efficiency or can you make death a glorious festival? It might only be for that fraction of a second but in that time you could write a trilogy. I used to love literature.

I think of each new dawn to come. It is as precious to me now as the forgotten process of my appeal. I do my best to not let my mind wander on this but when I lay down and look up at the sky and force myself to study it, it opens as much fascination for me as the memory of my bedroom in Dada's house and the yellow sunlight where Mo walks in the light of the shutters with his long swishing strides.

If you study one particular spot you learn about your place in the world, the accident of history, the importance of home or night, the joy of imagining other seas and continents and shores. We are lucky here south of the equator. We can imagine that other life much easier when the sky turns to green and you know another day is coming to an end and your thoughts flow automatically towards the dawn. The electric in the night in the dry seasons echoes the electricity in my brain, the movement of blood through my heart, a vast internal seaway with its own ports and rivers and quaysides and me, knife in hand, jumping along its banks.

Here comes the manifest, the loading of the cargo, the pillaging of spices and jewels from the river boats of these islands. What we Sea Dayaks do best when we are forced to look back to our history. I can still echo though my heart what would cease to beat. These pictures in my head bear their own reality instead but it is in vain. No matter how my thinking, the enormous grey of the dawn is still there before me and no matter how I try in the green empty luminosity of the night, my appeal lies in tatters. Sometimes it is easier to let my thoughts settle into their natural own groove rather than trying to follow them elsewhere. We are a sea going people. We understand the waves and those who live upon the water.

'When they come to kill you and with the blessing of God' I hear again Shabela's voice. It comes accompanied by Mo's laughter; Iskra is there with his heavy boxer's forearms and the phrases he turns into jokes.

They always come for you at dawn, that's what I know; to get the thing done early so everyone can get on with their day and the sun cross its line. I don't like surprises. When something is going to happen I want to be ready. I got to taking extended naps through the day whenever the time is quiet, in order to keep guard over the night. To be aware of the first few lines of the grey, the hint of daybreak in the dark dome above, the peeling away of the stars; the disappearing light of the moon gone to the sea brings me a strange, deep, freedom, like a shifting of the earth itself...

This is the time they come. I wake just once after midnight and can swear there are voices, I listen intently, my ears cocked for any sound. If they are coming and you can see yourself going with them to die and know they will return to have their breakfast and you will be dead, it leaves a funny feeling inside you, an unsettling middle passage. It's like when you lose something and try to retrace your steps, and imagine being in the same place a moment earlier, what has changed, you or the situation? Approaching death is the same. They do a lot of imagining in this place. I want to be prepared. What do the sounds of your step sound like to them when they take you? Can you imagine a dead man's footsteps returning to the same cell door like a never ending wave? Just the thought makes you nauseous.

Things I don't like to talk about don't worry me now. I

can see and hear those steps when the guards return to have early bowls of noodles with beef a green leaf for decoration and orange gravy and leave a body in their wake. Dada used to say that no matter how bad your condition there is always something to be thankful for, there is always someone worse.

Each morning when the sky brightens and you can see some clear sunshine before the rain and the light invades my cell, I know he's right. Even the faintest rustle sends me to the door, my ear pressed to the rough, cold wood and listening so intently that all I can hear is my breathing pulse through me like an ocean. I'm profoundly grateful and thankful that no one is going to come now except the Cook and the boy with my breakfast.

I have another twenty four hours of freedom. They gave my Dada two years to spend in prison for sedition but his corrective stain lasts a lifetime. It falls across the family like a shroud but the patriot game is not for him. He does not see the same borders as the rulers but he gets the joke. Like everything around here the jokes are never about what they are really about. The stories of muddied blood seep around him like a seaway; his punishment, to deter others.

There is to be no final appeal. The holy man doesn't need to tell me this. I will still make the most of the idea until it sinks me. I used to amuse myself by thinking of all those resounding phrases that I would issue that would ring around the court room on my behalf. It would be cooler in there as well, studying the effects of each resonant note so as to extract the most consolation from the judge while the air conditioner clanks and groans and the holy ones shudder.

'Your Dada has completed his punishment but expect nothing from them,' the lady in blue says.

She is the polished jewel of his troubled history; always around me at these terrible moments, like the three nails of the cross. Her eyes shine the same as mine as if she is sharing some huge joke with me; and always, always the blue in her earrings and silver within the fabric of her clothes as if to denote the mixture of her blood across this scarred land.

'You will be taken to a place and there hung by the neck until death'.

It is common knowledge I say to myself that life isn't worth living anyway, it's too much of a struggle. What does it matter if you die at twenty three or eighty three; there is only another sixty years to get through. Seeing things this way life does not seem so bad.

Iskra can have his next forty years of pimping before his skin turns to parchment and his hands begin to shake like old Srino's. I have slept with men and women, rolled the dice and dipped the crystal rock; blown out smoke like from a trumpet and sipped all the clear liquid drinks I could take. I have worked at my trade and smelled the river each morning instead of letting my life go by. It is better far better than sitting behind a desk or tiring my brain with voluminous studies. Men and women will continue to go on living, families will struggle, death comes for each one of us, this business of dying just has to be got through, the holy man is right on that score. But you still fight it just like you have to fight being born...

Everything is a journey. The thought of another forty years of life, of laughing and getting high, of parties and work, sunshine and sleep seems like a never ending celebration. I want it. I want it more than anything on earth, as surely as the sea or the stack of summer days that can be extracted from the bud or like a bee sucks pollen from a flower or the sweetest orange plant or a monkey that paws a bunch of yellow fruit taken direct from the bark of a Beccaria tree but it is not to be given to me.

Chapter Three

The trial concludes

The finish of the trial comes like a song; the conclusion to a drama, the end of a rainbow being slowly emptied into the sea, blown away by the sound of the wind and incessant rain. But I'm wrong. The finish does come with certain stillness but accompanying that stillness is the mad bedlam of the labyrinth. It makes me wonder who is really on trial. Am I as much of a traitor to Malaysia as my Dada? Is it me holding a triangle in a great orchestra or an egg cup of water in a roaring river? Only the State can decide now if I am allowed any say. It is always interesting for the prisoner in the dock to hear himself being talked about. And certainly in the concluding speeches of my lawyer and the prosecuting council there is a great deal more said about me, than I know myself, more about my person than my crime.

In reality there isn't much difference between the two lawyers. Counsel for the defence raises his arms to heaven, speaks about my 'deprived' associations and asks for guilty with extenuating circumstances. The prosecutor make a similar gesture but asks for the guilty plea and maximum sentence not only for a callous murder but also for my depraved life as a sodomite and subterranean.

'A sodomite, a sodomite,' he repeats with certain vigour and then almost in a whisper,

'One with a supine and traitorous character; there is nothing "extenuating" about his circumstances, neither in his circumstances nor in his culture,' he says.

One thing about these opposing views is very irritating, quite often when being spoken about so much I am tempted to put a quick word in but my lawyer expressly forbids it.

'It would do you more danger than any good' he says.

'You won't improve your case by speaking out,' he warns.

In fact there seems to be a conspiracy to keep me from opening my mouth. Are they scared of what I have to say; my fate decided out of hand regardless of the things I don't like to talk about. Do they not want to hear about this fucked up island and its history or that we Sea Dayaks like to feel the sun upon our faces and are not made for farming but running these waters in junks and sampans and gigs, that we plunder and come back to our villages to lie in hammocks and watch the sky. We are the vagabonds the State despises.

Our time is not to be measured by the fields or the passage of the great lighted ball around the earth but of the moon, the night and the pull of tides. We are as unusual as the Chinese who have traded here for a thousand years but we are here first and our primary love is of the blessed rivers and Straits, ours is a furious history until the Sultans, Malay and White wrapped us like silk around their golden wrists or even that the Chinese even give our city its name.

At times it is quite an effort for me not to not cut them short and say;

'Shut your blasted traps. Who is on trial anyway? Does your prisoner have any say in what is going on here?

'It is me sitting in the dock on trial for murder, can I not speak?'

On reflection I have nothing much to say. It would make little sense to them. Hearing yourself being talked about so often makes you soon lose interest or bother to listen for legal points that so consume them. It is too much of an effort within that heat with everyone sweating until the air conditioning gets turned so high that the cold runs through the court like a knife and some of the jury start to sneeze. I think instead of the nurse at Dada's funeral with her bruised face and the movement that shakes her headscarf, the cooler would then go back to its own lumbering uncertainty and we would all sweat again. Under those circumstances is it any wonder my attention starts to wander.

The prosecutor tries to make his speech dramatic but I had looked away before he was half way through. The only things that really catch my attention are occasional phrases being levelled against me then with a sudden switch of gear, he moves towards some new and elaborate point.

These shifts in focus make me think of the way you can see the trees that line my Dada's retirement village or the colour of the beach and the rose yellow and green huts and the black outcrop of the rocks that the Kalimantans had hidden behind as we searched for them.

The colours bring me back, sand, trees, air, I can see them now.

The prosecutor says he can show that my crime is pre-meditated. An action ordained rather than the extenuating circumstances my defence has put forward.

'A sin of omission!' he snorts in derision.

'No one speaks of pure chance on this side of the Bar,' I remember him saying at one moment,

'I can prove his culpability to you, ladies and gentlemen of the jury. The facts of the crime are as clear as daylight. We have the weapon, we have the prosecution witnesses, but more importantly', he leans forward, 'we have the character of a man who possesses a criminal and traitorous mentality even before his use of the knife.

'A man who consorts with the dark side of the night and the people who are drawn to it, a violent dangerous place into which these poor white tourists stumbled and which thankfully as a nation we have tried to rid ourselves of, these iniquitous dens the accused and his friends inhabit.'

He does not need to say that the Chinese run the bars, all the allusion and litigation, he sips like wine, are there in his words, a conjuror of images.

He starts to sum up the facts from the day of my Dada's death but it is not me he's talking about.

'I have described to you the series of events which leads this man to kill his victims when he is fully aware, he has even admitted to you himself, the effect of that cacophony of drugged madness wearing thin within him until all that is left is mere irritation then revenge.

'This man knows the actions he commits when he embarks upon this journey; fully aware of the consequences' he repeats himself.

'We are not concerned here with an act of homicide committed on a sudden impulse and with one single and fatal stab which might serve as an extenuation of the circumstances but a sustained and prolonged assault along a path already chosen.'

The prosecutor wipes his brow.

'We know the prisoner is a criminal, but we also know he was educated at the high school, until he chose to leave. He is not without some education. You will have observed the way he answers my questions. He is intelligent enough and he knows the power of words. It is quite impossible to believe that he has committed these crimes without being aware.'

The intelligence that I supposedly possessed is now used against me; any solidarity with my Dada is merely a construction in the use of narrative to show the overwhelming manner of my guilt. I miss what he says next except that when I look up I hear him exclaim in a manner of exaltation, the way tourists sometimes greet the sunsets over the river after the rain, a sort of hallelujah of righteous indignation that becomes almost a whisper.

'Gentlemen and Ladies, not once in these proceedings does this man utter the least act of contrition.

'We know what sort of character his Dada possesses, a man of obduracy, and a Chinese communist who could have wrecked these islands by his actions,' he continues.

'What about my mother and father,' I shout, 'aren't they good Malaysians?

'Are they not responsible; the way they shun the Dada and say that within him there resides the child of the comprador and white oppressor, kindled by the Chinese. Are they not somehow to play a part in his downfall by saying only that his own bitterness and egocentricity leads to his failing health?'

I spit this out in a rare mood of defiance. The judge rebukes my counsel.

My poor mother shudders in the court house. She sits next to the woman in blue who nods as if everything being said has a ring of truth. The two women hold hands; an empty space echoes my father's absence.

'Please instruct your client to be quiet. His comments are to be struck from the record,' the Judge says. My lawyer nods in agreement.

The prosecutor speaks up, 'Here we have an example of this man's heartlessness. Is there any word of sympathy for his victims in that last soliloquy? Is there one moment of doubt given for their suffering families? He does not even know the age of his grandfather, the visit to the bathing pool with *his friend*, the purpose of the visit to the pictures, a day at the beach house with an outsider and his *good* wife who by the grace of god is not witness to the last fateful scene; are not all these the action of a pimp, two poor boys left dead within his orgy and a lover subject only to his criminal gratification?'

His voice sinks as he rehearses again the laws of this land and the offences committed between men who abuse that silver writ.

He turns quickly as if to move away from those who have helped in this judicial proceeding to my friend Iskra. Here he shows a certain deftness, a card sharpers speed, away from the 'crimes' Mo and I have committed in our time together and back to the perpetrator's other friends. Every utterance he makes sounds quite plausible; it is true about the letter written in collusion between myself and Iskra so as to entice his mistress to his room.

But to call him a 'dark creature of the night, one who deals with drugs and with women and sordid cafés as if he has been born to them.

'No' the prosecutor says, 'No, it is not to exaggerate.'

Swimming with drugs but connected to reality I have provoked a brawl with Iskra's enemies in the course of which my friend is wounded, and then I ask for his knife with one sole intention. I drive with him and Mo to the city in a night full of wind, stars and rain and purposely engineer a fight with the two poor white boys, because in my own bitterness, when they refuse my advances, I challenge them and hunt them down like animals and do not stop before mercilessly slaying one then the other.

'That is my case,' the prosecutor says.

Muddied blood is his next allusion. Turning towards the dock he points a finger at me and continues in the same manner. I really cannot understand why he harps on so much about this point but of course he has his reasons. I feel so tired, I don't feel much regret for what I have done, only tiredness. What has happened has happened. But the prosecutor taps into a certain history. The court room turns electric; the history of these islands is being examined. The Dada, no plaster saint, has frequented his own time, his ships and his women; he is not a pirate but he could have been; his grandson follows the example set by his own tortured soul.

Would I kill again? No I certainly would not but that is no longer the issue, the issue, the situation, the context is the place chance brought me to that night.

The slap across my face is the face of my own history. I have no regret in rising against it like the raising of my own black flag. But the hurt and rage are gone now; now is the time for parlay and reconciliation. The prosecutor is overdoing it, the way they all do here. I would have liked the chance of explaining to him in a friendly sort of way; to say it really isn't my fault that the whites who rule this place for so many years up to the war do not give a damn and even less for the Malays that follow them and then collude in their own subjugation.

The Chinese are always here but as long as they run the shops and the bars and the clubs the rulers do not care. When the Indonesians burn our boats we have to act superior because this is our place but it does no good to ape them because we Dayaks don't feel that way about anyone; especially when they roll out the red carpet for the Malay nation with its laws and state and parliament across the China Sea. It is that the Dada hates. He does not want to be Chinese or White or Malay or anything. A Borneo seaman is his bread and butter, a sea Dayak in his soul, the great Nana whom I do not know and his Malay wife who long ago crosses the water to Singapore.

The prosecutor is speaking again.

'We hear from his friend Mohammed that the accused says he can smell and taste blood, the blood of the powerful, the blood of the oppressor,' he pauses, 'by his own admission these are the words from the mouth of a sodomite.'

I wanted to be away from here, away, anywhere, off and sailing like the Dada across the sea but my mouth is glued. Nor can I tell anyone that nothing matters.

The Dada says that the sea absolves all beliefs and the only wave you should ever pray to is the God without name, one god and one soul, one love above or below; to no one else give mention but love your neighbour. There is no religion south of the belly.

'I have never regretted anything in my whole life.' Dada used to say. I shudder now when I think of those words but they are all that matters, Wabu Sabi, the poetry of the moment.

Things happen and you react or you do not react, that is all. You live your life under the sun and the rain and the moments of every day that give you grace. I've always been too much absorbed in the present moment or the immediate future to look anywhere else. After my outburst there is never going to be a chance of being allowed to clear that up or speak again. The prosecutor now considers the inner life of my character. What he calls my lack of 'alma', an existence lived as a sin.

He says he has studied me closely and that he has found a blank towards those deep and inner feelings that normal people possess. There is no depth to me, no examined life, no feeling for my actions; none of those moral qualities normal people demonstrate every day.

'No doubt,' he adds 'we should not blame him for this, he is a poor fish dock worker, who possesses a roof only because of the generosity of his grandfather. We cannot blame a man for lacking what is not in his power to acquire. But in this criminal court every aggression must be tested against a series of higher principles, to the rule of law and justice.'

Gone is the fact now that I am intelligent. I am just a poor worker down on the dock like all the others. My mother stares impassively ahead. Once her eyes stray in my direction but for the most part she sits erect besides the woman in blue who slowly rubs her pearl earrings between her thumb and crook of her index finger .My mother dabs occasionally at her face when she does steal a glance; my poor, sweet, devastated ma.

'This man before you is a menace to society because in his own eyes he has done nothing wrong. He has enjoyed himself and now he stands before you by "chance!"'

The prosecutor quotes from certain dramatic novelists in the way I have pursued my victims.

'This man is a menace to our society.' he repeats again. The air conditioning has faltered and the jury are wiping the sweat from their brow in the late afternoon. Most crimes he tells them pale into insignificance besides the loathing inspired by my callousness to say nothing of the damage done to the wider reputation of these islands; how the modern world supplies so many tourists to our beautiful land.

'This man who is morally implicated in his grandfather's death and complicit by his own traitorous activity is no less fit to have a place in the community than those other men he resides with on the dark edge of our society.'

He returns to his unbroken necklace theme, my Dada's death, the fight on the beach with the Kalimantans, Iskra's wounds and the hunting down and killing of those two poor young men who have done nothing more than to be exorbitant with their voices. 'Contrast this to the murderous silence of the accused as he slowly drifts back to reality amid the paranoid gloom of the drug locally entitled…'

Here he takes a cursory look at his papers, 'Ya Bang, Ice, Crystal meth, Rock – Crack Cocaine, all words that the underworld choose as the lexicon of their depravity.

'Yes ladies and gentlemen I am convinced one siege led to another, just as one fishing boat follows another to the sea that brings those two poor souls to our island and leads to their early demise by this murderous son of Sarawak.' He raises his voice a tone,

'You will not find I am exaggerating the case against the prisoner when I say that he is guilty of a series of murders, to be sentenced by this court. I look to you for a verdict accordingly.'

The prosecutor pauses to wipe the sweat off his face. He then explains that his duty is a painful one but one he would not flinch to undertake.

'This man has no place in the community whose basic principles of law he flouts without compunction. Nor heartless as he is, has he any claims to mercy. I ask you to impose the extreme penalty of the law and I do so without qualm. In the course of a long career in which it has often been my duty to ask for a capital sentence, never have I have felt that painful duty to weigh so lightly on my mind as it does with this case. It demands a verdict of murder without extenuating circumstances. I am following not only the dictates of my conscience and sacred obligation but also the sentiment of a natural and righteous indignation that sweeps across our land.'

When the prosecutor sits down there is a silence. It seems to convey a greater resonance, a meaning beyond shock. The heat and the drone of his voice have gone over me but I sit up straight at what I have been hearing. That is not me he is talking about but a shadow, some lurid memory of his own imagination, and to roll myself and the Dada into the same traitorous crimes against the nation; well that is criminal. Is it only for me to study the line and silver threads woven into the fabric into the lady's blue skirt who sits next to my mother?

The presiding judge gives a low cough and asks me in a short stentorian voice if I have anything to say. I rise and say I had no intention of killing those tourists. The judge replies that this statement will be taken into consideration by the court. Meanwhile he would be glad to hear before my counsel addresses the court, to explain again the motives of my crime. So far, he has to admit, he has not fully understood the grounds for my defence.

I stand again and try to explain the heavy culmination of the day's events, the sun, the water, the food and drugs and how I'd woken that morning with my mouth bitter and confusion in my head, then the fight with the Kalimantans and the car ride to the city beneath a wet moon. I point at the prosecutor,

'What does he know of such things? If I am a mix of blood, this lawyer refers to, is it not the same blood across all this island and is there not enough of it mixed between ourselves in our lives together here.'

I speak quickly but my words roll into one another and clash like stones. I am conscious that what I am saying sounds incoherent even though I know it to be true. I hear a gentle laugh come like a sea breeze across the courtroom. I look up and see a jury member cover her mouth. She flutters a green silk handkerchief across her nervous fingers and I see Mo holding the silver paper like a grill. The woman in blue looks at me as if to say, 'I told you so.'

My mother shudders.

I do not sing my father's song nor ask for mitigation for his corrective purges, nor do I point to his absence across the court room or accuse him with his lash and doleful acts of 'contrition'. I will not confide before them my terror when I hear his soft footfall on the stairs nor demean myself to sit quietly; let them accuse me of my own persuasions. I will face them all.

My lawyer shrugs his shoulders and tugs at his cuffs. He is directed to address the court. All he does is to point out the lateness of the hour. As he indicates his watch one of his cufflinks shines a wan gold. It could be bullion for the old pirates like a European clipper ripe for picking or a Chinese sampan waddling like a duck up the straits of Molucca. He asks for an adjournment until the following afternoon. The judge nods.

Chapter Four

Legal Loopholes

When they bring me back to Court the air conditioning is fully functioning. It needs to be. Even from the prison van I can feel the brightness of the sky and the heat that seems to penetrate even the metal grilles. It does not matter. As if by rote, the members of the jury are fanning themselves in some sort of expectant rhythm. The speech for the defence seems to me interminable. At one moment though, I prick up my ears.

I hear my lawyer say, 'Yes it is true I killed two men.'

He refers to me as if speaking of himself. It seems so strange .I do not understand but bend to one of the policemen at my side.

'What is he playing at?' I raise my head in the brief's direction. The policeman tells me to shut up. After a moment he whispers.

'They all do it, it's called transference. They take on the fact that the jury think it is you speaking, and they are looking at you but it is him speaking. Did you ever see all that stuff they used to do on the fairgrounds years back? These fellers are not a patch on those.'

It seems to me as me if they want to exclude me from the case. I want to jump up and say, 'this is me, the Sea Dayak' but it doesn't seem to matter. I don't want to be slung down again. But the lawyer is a poor ventriloquist, an even poorer image maker and nobody seems to believe what he has to say anyway; whoever he thinks he is. I feel his words dribble away like water and see an image of the time at the beach house rise before me. He hurries through his plea of provocation but without much commitment and a lot less talent than the flowing phrases of the prosecutor.

'He knows me inside out,' he says. He has closely studied me he says.

He turns, 'Unlike my learned friend I have found something there. Indeed,' he adds,

'I may say that I have read the prisoner's mind like an open book.'

What he sees is an excellent young fellow, a steady conscientious worker who does his best by all around him, especially his employers at the fish market. If it had not been for an unfortunate set of circumstances at his parent's home and with his grandfather's troubled past he would have continued with his studies. He is popular with everyone and sympathetic to anyone's trouble. Accordingly as a dutiful grandson he has supported his grandfather when all turn away but knowing his time in prison and house arrest has weakened him, gives anxious consideration to where he can best place him and all his failings. Accordingly he undertakes to research the home up the river where the Dada passes his final days as a contented old man. Rana knows that his Dada needs more comfort and security than he himself can provide.

Even I am confused by now as to which corpus the lawyer resides, a place and time I do not like to talk about.

'I am astounded' he continues, 'by the attitude taken by my learned friend in referring to the heartless action of placing the old man in the home. Surely if proof is needed of the excellence of such places than we should look no further than on the policy of the government towards these institutions. They are part financed and promoted by State departments. The seamen in particular upon whom this nation depends also contribute towards them through their pensions. It is merely unfortunate that this Dada is the ringleader of that early union strike and could have ruined the incubus of our Nation's birth, with his talk.'

For all his long-windedness, the lawyer skips the funeral, nor does he mention the Dada's bad blood and misses the apex of argument that the prosecutor has used for my communist 'Chinese' Dada and his Catholic practices which had led to the strike and traitorous acts and to how much that influence has spilled over me.

My brain is shredded, Its membranes feel as if they were left out to dry in the sun or washed away in rivulets by the rain like a Rafaela's flower, as damp and apparently dead as its red and brown leather leaves in bitter contrast to the steady beating of its heart.

What with lawyer's long words, the endless days and hours, the stifling heat, that clamours through door and window for entry I find my mind blurred and everything is slowly dissolving into a grey watery mess inside me. How well I now remembered the policeman's words, 'in the end it drains you'.

Only one incident stands out. Towards the end while my counsel rambles on, I hear the thin tunes of an ice cream cart in the street, a small jangling sound of bells and chimes that cuts across his flow of words and empty paraphrase. A rush of memories go rushing through my mind of the red sunsets in the dry season, memories of a life no longer mine but eclipsed by the actions of these two puppets of the State. Memories that have once provided me with the surest, humblest pleasures, the warm smells of summer, my favourite streets, the space by the water where the sky hangs low at evening, even the rain that brings a deeper green to the trees and a cooling balm like sandalwood to the air by the river; Mo's clean clothes and his laughter bubbling up through those bright teeth with his hair swept back. How beautiful it is. How beautiful he is.

The futility of what is happening seems to take me by the throat and to slowly throttle me. I have only one thought, to get it over as soon as possible. To get out and be in the space between the court and the police van when I can take my two breaths of freedom under the unmoving sky. This is my sole aim before the return to my cell and to sleep, sleep, sleep.

My lawyer has finished his peroration; only one verdict is possible he declaims that of homicide with extenuating circumstances. His voice drains away. The court rises and he sits down and looks exhausted. Some of his colleagues come up to him and shake his hand.

'A magnificent fight, well done' one of them says.

Another looks over to me to testify to the performance.

'Just fine that speech,' he indicates.

I nod my head but say nothing. I have nothing to say.

Everything seems so far away to know whether his performance has been good or otherwise. To me it's all the same.

The end of the day brings a heat that is not as intense. The late rains would arrive before dark. By the sounds that reach up from the street, I know that the cool of the evening would not be slow in coming. We wait. I expect the arrival of the police van for some signal. Everyone seemed to be waiting. I look around the courtroom, exactly the same as the day I first arrive. I meet the eyes of a journalist but he does not return my gaze. It reminds me that not once during the whole hearing have I tried to catch sight of Mo or share a message through our eyes.

I have not forgotten him but am just too preoccupied with other matters. I see him now. Two policemen sit at each side of him and separate him from Iskra, Srino and Shabela. He gives me a little wave as if to say, 'And with the blessing of God.'

'At last,' he seems to be saying. He is concerned to get things over with. He smiles but I can see the anxiety in his face.

My heart has turned to stone even without his testimony. I can accept him with a certain disregard now. I return his smile but it is an empty one. Then I think, how can I be so heartless, we are all strangers to each other, especially at night. He needs protection now.

The judges come back to their seats. The man in black reads a string of questions out to the jury. I catch a word here and there, malice or murderous forethought, provocation, extenuating circumstances. The jury retire and I am taken to the little room where I had already spent some time.

My lawyer comes to see me and sits near. He is very talkative. I wish he would shut up. He shows me more cordiality and confidence with his chat than he has ever done before. He assures me that everything would go well and that I would get off with a few years.

'The corrective service will rid you of the stain.' he says.

'Corrective Service like my Dada had to endure.' I say. 'That is what killed him even after his friends got him away to sea again'. He nods but says he does not know, as if he is thinking of something else.

I ask what are the chances of getting the sentence quashed as it only seems to be bad luck that my history rises before me just when the white boys are having their argument.

'Were they disturbing your peace?' He shrugs.

I remind him of the terrible slap that shook me.

'A heavy price,' he says.

'We all carry our history within us.' I say.

'No chance' he says. He has not raised any particular points of law as this might prejudice the jury one way or another. It is difficult to get a judgement quashed on anything but technical grounds and none of that exists here. I can see his point and in a way, I agree. If you looked at the matter dispassionately, two tourist deaths is not a point of view that you can share.

'In any case,' the lawyer says, 'you can appeal in the ordinary way but I'm convinced the verdict will be favourable.'

We wait around for quite a while, about three quarters of an hour. The policeman offers me another cigarette but I refuse. It seems strange now but I want to get back to my cell. Those two breaths of freedom still haunt me. I can feel the rain coming with the night. A bell rings and the lawyer takes his leave.

Over his shoulder he says, 'The foreman of the jury will read out all of the answers. You will be called on after that to hear the judgment.'

Doors bang. I hear people hurrying down flights of steps and a certain coolness when I know the rain must have come. The heat has diminished but still hangs in the air like a damp towel. It drapes itself upon me like that moment on the beach. I cannot tell if voices are nearby or distant. When I hear them still droning away in the courtroom I know something is up.

The bell rings again. I step back into the dock. The silent court room wraps itself around me. Even the lighting seems somehow dimmed. With the silence comes a strange sensation. I note that even the young smartly dressed journalist with the angular features, the one who has originally eyed me with such fascination, now turns his head to one side.

I do not look at Mo. I have no time even if I want to. The presiding judge starts with his pronouncements. I can see he wears his black cap, the one he has carried beneath his shoulder for the duration of the trial. In short they are to take me out and hang me, hang me by the neck until I am dead.

I feel like sitting down but pirates don't sit. They stand and stare. My sentence is no different from the thousands handed down to the stateless ones, the undocumented, the men and women who all hustle their lives from fishing boats and docksides. My life is just the same. My father says he wants me to face up to the chaos inside me but I am not alone. When they burn wood in Kalimantan it permeates across all the sad moments of this island. What a good citizen he is, my father. My death shall be his honour but I cannot help but shake inside.

I do not interpret the looks on the faces of the people present. The mood seems to be one of respectful sympathy. Sobs are coming from Mo's direction but I do not look up. The policemen handle me very gently too. The lawyer places his hand upon my wrist. I have stopped thinking and am held afloat merely by the smell of rain and the sky sailing above me. I hear the judge ask me if I have anything to say. After considering for a moment my mouth starts to open and I think to recite a string of epithets and curses that any pirate would utter at this moment of crisis. I see the lady in blue look up, her features sharp and drawn as a little mynah bird, her eyes brilliant with tears. She stares at me.

'The Sea Dayaks are my people.' I want to shout.

Instead I utter a decisive 'No.'

Chapter Five

Mo's Betrayal

Mo comes to testify. He wears a hat but quickly whips it off under the unrelenting glare of the prosecutor's eye. He enters the witness box. His head is shorn and bowed. Where is the lovely weave of his hair as it floated on the green water that Sunday? I want him with his hair returned. From where I am sitting I have a glimpse of his firm chest and the little undulations of skin above his hips. He appears very nervous and fiddles with his hat but in a different way than how Shabel holds his when he bends to look at me, 'And with the blessing of god.' Mo does not look.

The first question is how long has he known me?

'Since the time I walked from my office to the fish dock,' he replies.

The prosecutor asks him what the relations were between us.

He clears his throat and whispers, 'Intimate.'

Answering another question, he nods when it is put to him that this intimacy is against the laws of the land.

The prosecutor who has been studying a document in his hand, asks him rather sharply, when our 'liaison' had begun. Mo gives the precise date.

The prosecutor then observes in a rather casual air,

'This would be around the time of the accused Dada's funeral would it not?'

'The day afterwards,' Mo says.

After letting this sink in, the prosecutor remarks in a slightly ironic tone, that given the laws of the land and this 'delicate' topic, he can sympathise with this young man's feelings but, here, his voice grows deeper in his throat, his duty obliges him to waive considerations of delicacy.

'We are a stern but fair nation,' he says as if taking a leaf from my father's book.

After making this pronouncement he asks Mo to give a full account of our doings on the day I forced myself upon him and we had intercourse. Mo does not answer at first but the prosecutor insists. He then tells told Mo that only by agreeing to the proceedings before the Magistrate could he be helped. Mo says that we met for the second time at the public baths, and then had gone together to the pictures and back to my Dada's house that night.

The prosecutor informs the court that as a result of certain statements made by the prosecution witness before the magistrate, he has taken this opportunity to redeem himself.

Turning to Mo, he asks slowly and carefully, 'How many times did the prisoner use the knife on the young white tourists?'

'Once, twice and three times sir,' Mo whispers.

'Once and twice for the first man and three times for

the second;' Mo nods. The prosecutor then takes the jury through the events that have unfolded that night at the waterfront.

'When is it you realise things have gone too far and that you must give evidence against this man?' the prosecutor asks.

Mo nods.

'When?' he persists.

'Crystal does strange things,' Mo says, 'it made Rana taste blood.'

Looking very grave the prosecutor draws his small frame up to his full height as if standing on a rock and with his robes gathered around him states.

'Gentle souls of the jury I would have you know that this man who stands before you in the dock is a criminal of the highest order and sentence of the highest order should be placed against him. That is all I wish to say.'

When he says this you could drop a pin into the stillness of the courtroom.

He sits down to the same dead silence. Then all of a sudden Mo bursts into tears. He's got it all wrong he says. It is not like that at all, no one has forced themselves upon him. The law has bullied him into saying the opposite of what he means to say. He knows me well and he knows in his heart I am a gentle character. At a sign from the presiding judge, one of the court ushers leads him away. The hearing continues.

The prosecutor is not finished. He jumps to his feet and again drapes his gown around him and says he is amazed at the disingenuous way the defence has been taken in by these so called friends of the accused.

'Each one of them would turn their evidence if offered

a chance if they were here on trial today.' He looks directly at Shabela and Iskra.

'Only one has the decency to come forward and stand before you with an honest heart.' he says.

He looks with a staged pity at the weeping Mo.

Minutes later you can still hear the rack of sobbing from the gallery but I cannot look. It is like the weeping noise of the stream behind the hut that fateful Sunday; the gurgling sound of the woman in blue with her bright bird eyes who gushes out her truth to me like broken waters around a stone.

The prosecutor's words seem to take effect upon the jury and the public. My lawyer merely shrugs his shoulders and wipes the sweat from his forehead. You can see he is rattled. Mo's words have not been good.

The court rises in a sudden flapping of papers like crows rising off a field. As I am being taken from the courthouse to the prison van, I am conscious for a few brief moments of the once familiar feel of a spring evening out of doors, the cool and the rain that we could never escape but there is a lightening sky west of the river that springs from the waters of the south China Sea and momentarily sets everywhere pink in a beautiful rose. Slow river evenings like this one make our city easy to love.

Sitting in the darkness of the prison van, with the rain drumming on the steel grilles like some form of corrugated chorus, I know there will be a lovely sunset. With all that comes the characteristic sounds of the place I know, the buzz and thrum of the docks, the gangs swarming to the ships and those in from the country for the night markets walking through the dusk. This certain hour of the day I have always enjoyed and walked home with dreams of food, satellite TV and rain. The shouts of newspaper boys call in slang , dressed in plastic to cover their shorts, their papers protected, the screams of the gulls on the wharf or starlings in the city gardens, the cries of the hot noodle stalls and squeal of the trolley buses that run between the water and the central districts, the sounds that come down from the upper town to my prison and how they meet with the noise of the single story houses that rise up from the suddenly still harbour all come to form a sort of whispering chorus that delights me then becomes quieter until darkness forces itself down and night begins.

The prosecutor's words and the thought that all my friends would testify against me runs like the beat of a drum through my insides. I suppose when you look at it what else could they say? Shabela knows they are watching him for drugs, Iskra is down for pimping and distributing, even Jalima, who they tap into for association and waltzing the tax at the restaurant. I am glad the woman in blue has been declined. Sometimes a defence is worse than a prosecution. This lawyer is a bag of tricks and venomous as a snake. And Mo, poor Mo, they will have him for the most heinous act on this island, an accomplice to an act of sodomy, a sodomite, an infidel unless he squeals. They'll throw him to the wolves if he spends a day in prison or if his buttocks are lovingly exposed to await the singing lash in the manner of which they like to administer justice here. None of them are to blame for my situation which the prosecutor terms, their 'confessions'. They turn to that on this island; make everyone keep watch against each other. The pirates and Dayaks in their brutality are the only ones with honour here; small wonder that the Rajahs have to put them down.

Before I chose to live at Dada's, my father worked in the country on an estate where they process the palm oil. One day he brings a young man to the house, a Kalimantan whose eyes alone could tell you of the distress he has suffered. I could hear him sobbing in the spare room like Old Srino used to weep in his kitchen before the birds started to sing. My father is missing for some time since we had eaten our dinner. My mother turns her face away. She puts her hands in her lap. When I ask for my father she shakes her head.

'I am sure he is somewhere' she says. 'I expect the Indonesian has been misbehaving again.'

'Your father has been very kind to those who come to work on that estate.' she says.

'He has told me the secret of my Dada's birth,' I say. She shudders. I do not realise until later that she thinks I know more.

I leave that house soon afterwards. The evening hour comes when I generally feel so well and look forward with contentment to sharing a bowl of rice noodles with the Dada and to listen to his stories. I would go to my bed with the sounds and smell of ships in my dreams and when the Dayaks parade, long haired and strong beneath the moon. It is the same hour but it is different now. Dada is dead and I am going back to my cell. What awaits me is a night full of foreboding and betrayals, the way in which Mo has been led down the path by the prosecutors questions which sanctify this blessed 'stern but fair' nation.

I trace the main features of these islands with my fingers across the cell wall then extend them upwards, north and west to the Philippines and down again as far south as Java, Sulawesi and what they used to call the Spices. I remember the fingers of the holy man and his signatures of the suffering.

I wonder where it is best to die, whether driven like a sailor across the sea or simply on a jungle floor beneath the trees. It is not only the northern hemisphere that reaches its soul to the stars but for prisoners like me to run their hands around their own freedoms or suffer the confinements of the stones. These islands are as much a prison cell to the innocent as a carefree sleep to a tourist who swings peacefully in a hammock under a starlit sky. You die anyway.

Chapter Six

The Witnesses

I can honestly say that one season quickly follows the other in quick succession. No seasons change as many lives as they do here, the days warmer or cooler, rainier or with less rain. The monsoon of November is very different from the one of May. As the warmer days approach I sense that something new is awaiting me. My case is due in the last session of the crown Court which finishes the concluding days of the month. The proceedings open with the sun blazing outside the courtroom. My lawyer assures me that it wouldn't last for more than two or three days, and besides he says the judges would be in a hurry because it's the start of the holiday season.

I know what he means. We are over the worst of the rain and our dry monsoon would soon be upon us. I love the beaches between April and September. We call them here the light yellow wine. There is more of sunlight even though you always have the downpour; the sun splits the days and brings us our evenings, like the light that fell that Sunday with all the huts along the beach glistening and groaning and an activity and abundance you can only imagine in November.

At seven in the morning, someone comes to get me and the police van takes me to the court room. Two policemen show me into a small room that smelled stale as if the windows had not been opened. On the other side of the door comes the sound of voices, names being called out, the scraping of chairs, voices of authority, the kind of commotion that makes me think of certain festivals we used to have in our district when they pull the furniture of the room to one side for dancing or when the bride first looks out of the window and flings her shift of flowers and the kids run free among the chickens.

The policeman tells me we have to wait to be called into the courtroom. One of them offers me a cigarette but I say no and show him the tiny piece of wood stuck between my teeth.

'I use these now' I say.

A little while later he asks me if I'm nervous. Again, I shake my head and say that in a way I'm quite interested in seeing a trial. I had never been in court before.

'I don't believe you,' he laughs.

I say it's true and he laughs again but I just shake my head and say no, not a in a serious one like this. Those other times were minor matters. This is the real thing.

'Yes,' says the second policeman, 'but a trial wears you out, it drains you. I've seen innocent guys fly away in their heads because they can't take it anymore. In the end they accept what they give you just to be rid of it.'

After a while a bell rings in the room. They take off my handcuffs and open the door and lead me into the dock. The room is jam packed. In spite of the blinds, bright sunlight filters through some broken slats. It is stifling hot. If they have left the windows closed for the air conditioning then something isn't working properly. Everyone is sweating.

I sit down and the cops stand on each side of me. It's then that I notice a row of faces in front of me. They are all watching me. I realise that they are the potential jury. They all look the same to me but I can see a scarf here and there, it is only later that I would be able to tell every feature of their faces line by line and what they seem to be thinking. It's a bit like getting on a bus or crowded train to go back to your district, at first there is just a sea of faces in front of you but after a while you realise the trace of each one there. They are all craning over to see me, the last passenger, and the accused: are they looking to see what is contemptible in the face of a killer? Do I really look like one? They used to call me baby face at school and in the early days on the fish dock but maybe there is something in me now that makes me look a monster. I do not really know.

It is confusing to have to face all the people crammed into this tiny space. Everyone seems to be talking and to know one another; I look around again but cannot recognise a single person. It has not occurred to me that most of the people here, all sweating, have just come to get a good look at the killer. No one normally takes any notice of me, especially on the markets when everyone is babbling and smoking before the rain. It takes some effort on my part to recognise that I am the source of all this commotion.

'There are so many people here'.I say to the policeman.

He tells me that it is because of the newspapers and points to a sea of faces sat at a table below the jury box.

'There they are.' he said. I ask who? And he replies, 'The journalists.'

'They are from Great Britain and Australia, the Daily Express, the Mirror, the Telegraph besides the Sarawak Weekly the Malay recorder and the Borneo Express.'

'What about the London Times?' I ask. He laughs.

'They say you are a psychopath,' he adds.

'They say you were high on drugs.'

'That is not exactly true.' I say, 'It is the coming down that screws you.' I do not mention the hallucinations.

'Is that going to be your defence?' he asks

'No,' I say, 'the slap of history is my defence. My reaction is just one of chance. If I had not been carrying the knife for a friend, this would not have happened.'

He looks at me and then away. Suddenly one of the journalists is coming towards us. The policeman knows him. He's Malay. He is middle aged and grimaces slightly when he puts one foot down on his right leg as though one favours another. It reminds me of the night of Dada's wake when all the residents of the home trooped and limped, sucking on their lips, into the room that held the coffin.

The journalist has a kindly face, not like the prosecuting judge who terrifies me with the cap beneath his arm he carries like a computer and his large book. He shakes the policeman's hand very warmly and again, I notice that everyone is talking in little groups, calling out to each other and chatting like in a club where everyone is happy to meet each other. They all have something in common, just like those bars that only serve coffee at half time or after the football because no one dares to order anything during the match.

I could not explain the circumstances why I feel totally alone. That everyone knows someone except me and they all have something together and I'm the intruder, maybe that is always the way it has worked. Nevertheless the journalist speaks to me and smiles. He says it he hopes the case would go well for me. I thank him and he adds, 'You know we've written widely about you. Your case has exercised the imagination, the soul and underbelly of our culture.'

I don't understand what he means. He says the trial would not last long.

'The turn of the seasons after May is the only time when the judges can get away. They never fail to have a rest after the major trials and then come back refreshed for the slow season and the winter monsoon.'

'I wouldn't worry,' the journalist says.

He then points out another small Malay man who is standing with the group that he has just left. He wears enormous glasses that look like those artificial ones with wobbly eyes you can buy at the fairground; one of the places where old Srino used to take his parrot. He looks like he has not missed many meals.

The policeman tells me that he is a special correspondent from Kuala Lumpur and has come especially for my case. It is important that Malaysian justice is seen as incorruptible to the rest of the world.

'They have asked him to send in your story in double quick time.' he says.

I nod. To thank him for his consideration seems ridiculous. If Dada had been here, he would know just what to do. He is used to dealing with officials. The journalist gives me another friendly little wave and walks away. We wait for a few more moments in the stifling heat.

The fat journalist is like my father who fritters away those years of my childhood with his stream of useless orders. My studies are good; my citizenship and language flowering. I am a bright young fellow, my father's friends, teachers and other managers all say so. All would be well if it were not for the family stain; the boy's grandfather. To even discuss him is to give countenance to the traitorous manner in which the lawless treat our island. They take all our benefits and bring us little in return except for criminal behaviour and chaos. Are we not the laughing stock of the modern world with those head hunting tribes of the high interior and the residue of piracy lingering on our coastlines?

'This is how they think,' Dada used to say.

My lawyer arrives, flowing in his robes and surrounded by several of his colleagues. Straight away he goes over to the journalists and starts to shake their hands, even those of the foreign correspondents who previously, if they had noticed me at all, had only glared. They exchange pleasantries and laugh together, completely at ease. Then the bell rings and everyone takes their place in court.

My lawyer comes over, shakes my hand and advises me to reply to any questions as briefly as possible. He asks me not to offer any additional information and to count on him to do the rest.

To my left I hear the sound of a chair being scraped across the floor a and the tall man, dressed all in red and with steel rimmed spectacles, which he constantly removes and replaces from his nose with a hand bearing a heavy gold ring on its final finger, sits down. The black cap sits beside him, borne by the clerk of the court.

Below and to the right side of the presiding judge, the chief prosecuting lawyer carefully lowers himself into his seat. He folds his robes beneath him as if he is sitting on a cushion. I struggle to remember any of the previous conversations with the Chinese detective. He definitely would not wear that sort of ring. He is far too courteous, not a show pony, he would not mock you with his power.

The clerk announces that the court is in session and at that very moment, the air conditioning cranks and slowly lumbers into action, filling the chambers with its groan. The judges, two of them in purple besides the one in red come into the courtroom with their files and very quickly take their places on the high platform. A small man in a black robe sits very rigid on the chair in the middle and places his own cap on the bench in front of him. He wipes his small head with a pale blue handkerchief and echoes the clerk of the court in declaring the proceedings officially open.

The journalists already have their pens in their hands and all wear the same slightly mocking looks on their faces. This is particularly true of the foreign correspondents. I notice that the man from Kuala Lumpur is trying to effect the same facial, slightly bored expression as the Europeans. The exception amongst them is the one who has come over, who looks much younger than the others and who wears a blue silk suit and floral tie. He leaves his laptop computer in front of him on the table and turns his neck. He stares at me. On his angular face with its shadows and no trace of fat around his collar, I can see his very bright eyes examining me carefully, yet without expressing anything that I can put my finger on. I have the bizarre impression of looking at myself like looking through the lens of a movie camera, like I'm in a film of my own.

It is perhaps because of this framing and also because I do not understand the court procedures around me that I don't really take in everything that happens next; the way the jurors are selected, the questions the presiding judge asks my lawyer, the prosecutor and the jury, when all the their heads turn towards him at the same time. A quick reading out of the official charges which contain the names and places I recognise and some additional questions for my lawyer that he seems to brush off. He looks over at me and smiles. Then the presiding judge says we should move to a call of the witnesses. The clerk reads out several names. They catch my attention.

From amid the crowd of spectators I witness only as a shapeless mass, I now watch as each person stands up, one by one and goes out by a side door; the director and the guy who is the caretaker at Dada's Home, Iskra, Shabela, and Jalima, Mo. He gives me a nervous little wave. I'm surprised I haven't noticed him earlier; then the final defence witness, the friend of Shabela's wife, the woman in blue who says she can tell me my history with her eyes closed. She stands up when her name is called. I recognise her. My lawyer shakes his head. She is declined.

Thank God, I thank him again, my story can be told without her gushings. She sits next to my mother.

She wears a jacket and her hair is pulled back and she wears earrings in the same silver decoration as the stars that stud her skirt. She levels her eyes in the same precise way as she had when she told me I would come to a bad end. I remember Shabela who just laughs as though he is trying to remember something about her and Iskra who says another girl lived in our building at one time in the past.

I count the times I have seen her before my arrest and on occasion she offers me a warning, a presentiment, a prediction, at the beach hut, at the restaurant, and before that, the street. She is my oracle, staring at me with a purposeful look that brings back all those things that I don't like to talk about. They rub together in my mind like stones. Her gaze is very intent as though she has missed something in her understanding.

I can imagine the magazine open before her at the café, a pencil in her mouth; a gatherer of stories from the labyrinth and alongside her a list of programmes she says control us. She is different from my mother with her little whispers, pursed lips and the absences that go before me now, severe, unforgiving, and silent except when she issues her comments about the Dada and my father. My mother sits with her hands folded in her lap, as though all hope has gone with my behaviour. My poor sweet, devastated mother; they sit next to each other as though accustomed to do so all their lives.

'Many bad things have happened in both our houses.' she says.

I remember looking at her. The sea is combing in little buttered waves behind the beach hut.

'They took away my baby,' she whispers.

The presiding judge begins to utter his words. He orders that the official proceedings begin. He knows that he does not have to remind the members no matter how many emotions might be aroused; they must discount these in favour of the evidence. He says his role is to preside over the trial with impartiality and to consider the case objectively. The jury's sentence would be made in the spirit of justice and, in any case, he would clear the court room if good order did not prevail among the public. He would not need more than the slightest reason to do so. People from Europe would be following these proceedings and proper behaviour must be heeded!

Even with air conditioning grumbling away the heat seeps everywhere. I can see members of the jury fanning themselves with bits of paper or those who were judicious enough to have brought fans use them in uniform purpose. A constant rustling of paper pervades the courtroom. The presiding judge gestures to the black coated clerk who immediately orders bottles of water for the top bench.

My interrogation begins at once, the presiding judge questions me calmly and even it seems with a touch of cordiality. Once again they ask me to confirm my identity and in spite of my irritation, my profession. On the other hand I relax, because I thought why get irritable; it would be a bad day in Heaven to pass judgement on someone with a different identity especially on this island.

The presiding judge then begins explaining what crime has been committed and what I, the accused, have done. He turns to me every three sentences and asks if each statement has the correct bearing. Each time I reply 'Correct.' as I had done in the detective's office.

'Yes, your honour.' I say. One time I forget with all the heat and confusion and call him your Worship, then slip again and call him 'Your Holiness.' Everyone laughs.

It takes a long time because the presiding judge includes the minutest detail, from the beach house to the car journey, the club, the music, the lights, and the high intensity time before the final incident. He dwells greatly on these moments.

'This case is strung like pearls upon a necklace,' he says.

The details seem to take for ever. Periodically he peers at me over his glasses. The whole time he is speaking, the journalists are taking notes. I can feel the eyes of the little woman in blue watching me with intensity as sharp as Kim Song at my Dada's wake.

The frame of our identity is echoed in that nameless sea of faces as each look at me with their own separate sense of being. Then they turn one by one back to the presiding judge, who coughs and leafs through his file and rubs his glasses after every phase of questioning, all the time fanning himself and taking an occasional sip from his bottled water.

He then tells me he has to ask some questions which might seem unconnected to my case but which could perhaps have a significant bearing on the whole structure of the matter. I realise Dada's appearance in these matters must have been the same. I immediately feel very uncomfortable especially with my Mother sitting rigid, erect and scared in the courtroom. I try to do what my lawyer has first counselled me. To present a story that my emotions are aroused and I could not control them, that I try hard to temper my rage but that it keeps getting in the way like a filter is placed over the lens of a camera.

The judge asks me the reasons why Dada took to a

Home. When I say I work all the time and do not have much money, he looks at me as if another crime has been committed.

He asks if Dada's death has affected me personally and I reply that Dada and I had expected nothing of each other, but he told good stories and he made me laugh and it hurt me when he got weak and sick. We had both got used to our new lives. Mo would never have been able to stay if Dada had still been living there but I don't say that. My lawyer has told me not to bring that up. The presiding judge says he doesn't want to dwell on these affairs and asks the prosecuting lawyer if he has any questions for me.

The prosecutor half turns and without looking directly at me, states that with the permission of the presiding judge, he would like to know why I had carried on with my vendetta when the first young white tourist had dropped to the floor and I had continued calmly to kill his friend.

'No,' I say, 'no vendetta your Honour, the whole affair is one of chance, pure chance.'

In that case; the prosecutor reminds me, why have I taken a knife with me and why follow the other tourist with such determination when his friend has fallen. A matter of pure chance? he asks.

I nod my head and say yes, very clearly; pure chance, because it is part of the same moment.

The prosecutor then says in a short and terse voice, 'Very good that will be all for the present.'

I couldn't quite follow what comes next. After some more long and boring discussion between the lawyers and the bench, the prosecutor, and my counsel, the presiding judge now says the court will rise. There is an adjournment until the afternoon when further evidence will be taken.

Before I know what is happening they rush me out to the prison van which drives me back. They give me my midday meal. After a short time just enough to realise how tired I feel, they come for me again, back to the same room, confronting the same faces and the whole dance starts again. Even with the sky overcast and the trees waiting for the rain, the heat of the day has increased. With the air conditioning on its last legs, further fans have been procured and people's faces seem to wave towards them like fronds from a coral reef.

A soup of warm air staggers from the machines and writhes over the orange, yellow and blue of the women's head scarves. My lawyer and my friends all seem a long way away. Now I know what the prison guard means.

The young journalist and an older woman in the public gallery stare intently at me. I wipe away the sweat from my face, barely conscious of whom they are, when they bring the director of the Home to the witness box. They ask him if Dada has often moaned about me and the chief answers 'Yes.', straight off. He looks up to the older woman who is the caretaker's wife. She nods.

That doesn't mean much, all older people have grievances and anyway, the Dada probably means, his wretched Malay son in law when he says that. Would anyone ask about him? The judge then asks the director to be more specific. Does the Dada reproach me for sending him to a home up the country, an old man, weak and ill and so far from his district and city of Kuching? Again the director nods his head.

He says, 'Yes, to get rid of him.' No one asks him to qualify his answer.

The director talks of my calmness on the day of the funeral and asked what he meant by my calmness he lowers his eyes and stares at his shoes. I can see him now looking at me as if unsure of my identity. Then he says that he, the accused, does not want to see his Dada's body but instead sat around drinking coffee and leaves the village immediately after the funeral.

'All his tears have been shed, that's what he told me,' the director says.

Another matter perplexes him. One of the undertakers tells him that I do not even know Dada's age. After a short silence to allow the judge to make a note, he asks if the Director has been referring to the prisoner in the dock. The director seems puzzled by this and the Judge explains the formality of the question and why he is bound to ask it

The director nods his head.

Ask him about all those ships of the Blue Funnel Line, I want to shout. How can you put pressure upon me for someone else's life? The judge asks the prosecutor if he has any questions to put at this moment and he answers loudly, 'Certainly not, I have all I need here.'

His tone and his look as he glances at me are so naked with loathing that it makes me feel what I have not felt in ages, the same certitude when my father shouts and screams at me for not acting like a proper Malay and when he takes me quietly upstairs and beats me with the rattan cane. My mother passes the room and catches my eye as if to say, 'There you are, I love you but you know how he is.' She remains silent downstairs. I don't like to talk about these things but I am free now in the sight of their loathing. I feel a foolish desire to burst into tears. For the first time I realise how much these people hate me.

After asking the jury and my lawyer if they have any questions, the Judge hears the caretaker's evidence from the home. On stepping into the witness box, the man throws a glance at me and then looks away. Replying to the prosecutor's questions he says that I'd declined to ask them to open the coffin or to see Dada's body and that I had smoked and dozed and drank black coffee.

'He looks like he was out of it,' the caretaker says, 'as if he had been to a party and come up here without any sleep.'

I feel a wave of indignation spreading through the court room and for the first time I realise the fact that I might be guilty.

'Am I to blame because of the issue so cruelly given to me?' the Dada used to say.

They get the caretaker to repeat what he's said about coffee, cigarettes and the amount I have smoked. The prosecutor turns to me again with a look in his eyes. He smooths down his robe like a surgeon about to operate.

My counsel then asks the caretaker if he had not enjoyed a cigarette with me but the prosecutor draws himself high with indignation and his face twists in a sneer, 'I'd like to know who is on trial in this court. Or does my friend think that by some form of propinquity a witness for the prosecution might be coerced into speaking for the defence, that he will shake the evidence, the abundant and cogent evidence that is against his client?'

The judge tells him to answer the question.

The old feller fidgets a bit then says, 'Well I know I oughtn't to have done it.' he mumbles, 'But I did take a ciggie off him just to share a moment or two of companionship.'

The judge asks me to comment, 'Yes your honour,' I say, 'I did offer a cigarette. It seemed right to share at that time.'

The caretaker looks at me with a sort of gratitude, then after humming and hawing for a bit suggests it is he and his wife who have offered me coffee from the time of my arrival. The older woman bristles in the gallery.

My lawyer exudes triumph, 'The jury will appreciate the importance of this admission.' he says.

The prosecutor dances to his feet.

'Quite so,' he booms, 'but why doesn't the accused keep his cigarettes in his pockets and refuse a coffee out of his own sense of courtesy in the company of the dead. Any person of common decency should have refused. This prisoner, as I will demonstrate, respects neither the decency of life nor the laws of this nation.'

I think he sounds ridiculous.

The caretaker returns to his seat. When they call Dada's old friend, a court officer has to help him to the box. Kim Song states that although he has been a great friend of my Dada, he has met me only once on the day of his funeral.

'How did he behave on that day?' the prosecutor asks.

'Well I was more upset, I can tell you that,' Mr Song says, 'and far too upset to notice everything and being tired by the heat and everything. My grief sort of blinds me. It has been a great shock. My good friend and ship mate's death, in fact I fainted, so I hardly noticed the young fellow.'

The prosecutor asks him to tell the court if he's seen me weep. When Kim Song answers that his Dada only wept when he lost money, a murmur of small chuckles goes up through the court.

'It is probably the same with him.' He looks at me. 'But no.' he adds emphatically. 'I trust the jury will take note of this reply.' the prosecutor says.

My lawyer rises at once and asks Mr Song in a tone that seems overly aggressive, 'Now think well old man, could you not see the defendant trying his best to keep calm because of all the other things raging within his life – including the sad death of his grandfather?'

He does not allude to any close relationship with Mo. I can see the prosecutor make a quick mark with his pen onto paper.

'Can you swear he did not share a tear?' Kim Song answers again, 'No.'

At this some people in the court let out a little laugh and my lawyer, pushing back one sleeve of his gown, says sternly, 'This is typical of the way this case is being conducted. No attempt is being made to elicit the true facts here.'

Kim Song raises his head to make himself look taller. He appears to shout although in truth his voice comes out as a loud, hoarse, whisper that fills the room.

'He used to talk with his Dada about what a shit heap this place is.'

He suddenly laughs and shows his gums.

'About how we're all fucked up here because of the Kalimantan and Chinese and all those Thai fishing boats cunts and the Burmese slaves and the way the Malays run the place after the White Rajahs used to wipe their arses on them for over a hundred years; and because everyone shits on everyone else here, even the government has to decide who is up its bum or down the plughole.'

The court room gasps at these profanities but Kim Song only grinned.

'I am just saying what they used to talk about,' he says. The prosecutor, who has been making dabs of pencil marks on his file like a game of joined dots, suddenly looks up. He makes no comment but his eyes narrow like a hawk's and he seems to nod to himself at this traitorous turn of events.

A short break follows. My lawyer says that my case has its own sense of progression and appears to be going very well. Then they call my friend Shabela and introduce him as a witness for the defence.

Now and then he throws me a glance. He keeps squeezing his cap in his big hands. He looks as if he is dressed in his best suit, the one he sometimes wears on Fridays he says for effect.

'Yes we rent the house,' he says. His stomach pops through his shirt buttons. I become fascinated by this when he breathes. I can remember the last time, I saw him walking into the sea. They ask if he knows me well and he says, 'Yes, Rana is a good friend and with the blessing of God.'

They ask him to state what he thought of my character and he says 'Okay.'. When they ask him to explain what he means by this, he replies that everyone knows what 'Ok' means.

Am I a secretive sort of man? they ask, 'No,' Shabela replies, he wouldn't call me that and tells them how he'd seen me swearing when I saw the Thai fishing boat coming into the river even though he is mistaken there. He thinks me patriotic.

The prosecutor asks him if I always pay my bills on time. Shabela laughs and says he doesn't know.

'You'll have to ask Jalima that, she is the one that runs the restaurant but with me,' he says, 'he always pays on the nail.'

'What does he buy from you?' the prosecutor asks.

'All sorts of things,' Shabela says.

'All right.' The prosecutor is slightly put out. He asks him what he knows of the alleged crime that has been committed by the defendant. Shabela places his hands directly on the Bar and I can tell he has a speech all ready to go.

'To my mind it's all an accident or a bad stroke of luck.' he says. 'If you think about places and times, arguments like that can throw you off your guard and if you are in the wrong place,' He is about to continue but the judge cuts him short.

'That's all thank you.' he says from the bench. The heads of the jury all swing around towards him.

Shabela seems flummoxed. He draws himself up to his full height and he says he has not quite finished what he has come to this Court to say. The Judge tells him to continue but to make it brief.

Shabela only repeats that it has been a terrible accident and that I am a good buddy who only holds a friend's knife in order to keep him out of trouble. And with the blessing of God…

'That is as may be,' the judge observes, 'but we are not here to try such accidents of circumstance but facts according to law which runs like a silver thread throughout our history.'

Shabela turns and gazes at me. There are tears in his eyes. He really does care about me even if we have met just the once. His lips tremble as he looks as if to say, 'I gave it a try my friend, I've done my best. If it has not helped you, I am truly sorry.'

I don't say anything or make any movement but apart from Mo, I want to step down and kiss him in front of all the court.

The judge repeats his order and Shabela stands down and returns to his place among the crowd. He is like an overweight actor gone to sit amongst his audience. He seems unsure of himself as if this whole place is a foreign territory, the witness box, the dock, the bench where the judges sit. During the rest of the hearing he remains there, leaning forward, eyes turned down, elbows on his knees. He twists his cap in his hands across his huge girth.

Hardly anyone listens to Old Srino. He states that I am reasonable and even though much younger than himself we manage to talk together of a night. I am responsible and a good young man to have in the same building. He says I have always looked after him at the fish dock and been very good to him at the house about the trouble of his missing bird or the one time he's sick. He informs the Court about my kindness, or when in answer to a question about the Dada, he says that I am more like Dada's real son and that he treated me like one, more than his own daughter and son in law were to him.

'They are the real criminals.' he says who punished the Dada by never going to see them.

'You have to understand that,' he says.

'You've got to understand.' He repeats himself again

and asks them; 'Is it not the real crime that begets another, nothing happens without a cause?'

The prosecutor nods as if in deference to his age. The Judge tells Srino he can leave the dock.

Iskra stands up. He gives me a jaunty little wave of his hand and leads off by saying I am completely innocent. The judge rebukes him.

'You are here to give evidence, not your views on the case.'

'You must confine yourself to answering those questions put to you,' he says.

They ask him if he knows why the boys have been killed and what are his relations with the perpetrator. Iskra takes this opportunity by explaining it is he himself, not me, who has to ask the European tourists to be quiet, to sit down and honour our customs.

'I do not mean this,' the prosecutor's eyes narrow again.

'What of this letter that has led to this train of events?' He waves a string of papers above his head.

'Ah nothing.' Iskra says. Some Indonesians have a grudge out for me because I beat up the guy's sister.

'How is it then that this letter leads directly to the tragedy and is the work of the accused?'

The prosecutor asks this as if I had shipped Dada off to the home just to establish Mo in the house, as part of some elaborate plot.

'By pure chance.' Iskra says.

'He does me a favour. I take him and his friend to the beach. A bit of a scuffle breaks out and I get a bit of a nick. He takes the knife off me when I want to chase the guy. We only took the drugs as a diversion because it has been a fidgety, troubled sort of day, the rains come after the sun and we all return back to the city. The music wafts over us. We're laughing; it is only by chance that we end up at that club on the waterfront. We are going to stay later at the beach hut with Shabela.' He looks to the gallery to where the big man nods and continues to fidget.

'We don't know who is going to come after us. Those who are shouting and slap us take us for fools, takes us away from our party, that's all, a chance thing.' He shrugs his wide shoulders.

'Two white boys lie murdered.' the Judge says.

The prosecuting barrister jumps to his feet.

'Chance or mere coincidence plays a remarkably large part in this tissue of lies,' he exclaims.

'Is it by chance that the prisoner has not intervened when this man assaults the girl who is his mistress? Does not this convention account for the accused's actions at the police station when summoned to make a statement? No.

'And now we find that "chance" again leads to the night club and to the knife and the killing of these two poor souls who wished only to visit our island and explore its rare beauty.

'What do you do for a living?' he asks Iskra.

On describing himself as a warehouseman who is temporarily out of work, the prosecutor informs the jury that it is common knowledge that the witness lives off the immoral earnings of illegal Burmese and Indonesian girls and that he supplies drugs around the district which he procures from the Thai fishing boats, eighty per cent of whom we all know are illegal.

'The accused,' the prosecutor says. 'is this man's close friend and confidant. In fact the whole background to this crime is of the most squalid form of disreputable association. Demeaned illegal women bought and sold for sex, drugs, liquor, parties and finally the extinguishing of two bright European lives who arrive from the home of democracy and have lived lives whom we know had soared like stars, so now cruelly terminated by a fish dock worker with a knife owned by a pimp.'

He wipes a bead of sweat away from his clammy forehead and continues.

'What has made this crime more malicious and odious is the personality of the man in this dock, an inhuman monster in that small face and frame, who exists solely without any sense of morals. What chance is there for any repentance in that?'

He is about to finish but mutters something of 'Bad blood.' as if passing a covert message around the court room.

'This nation cannot be too careful,' he says. 'we know this from our history.'

Iskra begins to splutter and I can see his hairy arms bunch tight. My lawyer is also expostulating. They are told that the prosecutor must be allowed to finish his remarks.

'I have nearly done.' the prosecutor says in a tone of mock weariness. He turns again to Iskra.

'Is the prisoner your friend?'

'Certainly, we are the best of pals as they say.'

The prosecutor then puts the same question to me. I look hard at Iskra and he does not turn away but looks me direct in the eye.

'Yes.' I say. The prosecutor turns with a glance to the bench but his full face to the jury.

'Not only does the man before you in the dock indulge

in the most shameful of acts, of which we shall hear later, but on the days following his grandfather's funeral, he moves his lover into his apartment then kills two young men in a furious cold blooded act. This is no doubt, in pursuance of some sad vendetta that he has built inside his head concerning the history of this island and located within his own unhappy family.' His voice rises.

'He conducts these acts in the underworld hell of iniquity of drugs and clubs and pimps and prostitutes. A life that is foreign to ninety-nine per cent of Malaysians. That, my gentle jury, is the type of man that this court is set to try before you today. You shall judge him by the category of his friends.'

No sooner does he sit down than my lawyer out of all patience and frustration, raises his arms so high that the sleeves of his gown fall back to reveal the full length of his shirt cuffs and gold cufflinks.

'Is my client on trial for having buried his grandfather, or for killing two men?'

There are titters in court as a handkerchief falls out of his sleeve onto the floor. The prosecutor springs to his feet.

He is amazed he says at the disingenuousness of his learned friend. His case has fallen as surely as his accoutrements. The court laughs again but the judge bids silence. Could the court not see that between these elements of the case, hangs a vital thread that links the Dada 'A funeral, the pimp's letter and the prisoner's final action?'

'In short,' he concludes and speaking with great vehemence says, 'I accuse this man before you in his behaviour and in all the vital elements that show he is already by his very nature, by his lack of remorse and his overt character to be a murderer at heart.'

He draws himself as high as Kim Song has done and concludes, 'A murderer to the dead, as much as the ideals of life among these great islands and peninsulas, we hold so dear.'

'What is more,' his voice came as little more than a whisper now, 'I shall demonstrate before you in the habitus of a common clerk all that is wrong in this court room today and all that is wrong with this man and all that is wrong with the stain left upon his poor family who only by the caring actions of his parents, have prevented more acute harm being done to the strong federal structure that we enjoy in this country today.'

He continues with this narrative of betrayal and subterfuge, of Dada as a communist sympathiser who leads out the seaman of this island at a crucial moment of this nation's destiny and his hold upon me. Blood is at the heart of this matter.

'Exhibit A.' The prosecutor gestures and holds out the knife in its plastic folder before him, 'Is the murder weapon.'

He points to me. 'And there before you is the murderer.' I see the woman in blue turn towards me. 'A baby passed over.'

Chapter Seven

Time as ally

Awaiting trial I look forward to the daily walk around the prison yard or the visit from my lawyer. As for the rest of the time, I am used to it and think even if I have to live inside any old hut in the forest I would have got used to it. The window in my cell brings me the sky and the ocean smell of the mangroves, the blinding morning light, passing clouds, the dawn with its soft smells of gardenias are all open to greet me. The rain falls down on the roof, the sun grows and the faint hum of the traffic roar rises from the city just at the time of my breakfast. It delivers to me another portion of the great life lived outside. The days are becoming warmer and there is a sweet breeze from the sea.

These sounds and smells are awash with every meal they bring me and memories from both inside and outside. Those I like most come from the horns and hooters of the passenger ships that adorn the harbour. They linger within me for hours. I love that. You can get used to anything that lights your memory or history.

When you accept you are a prisoner things change. Knowing you are a criminal brings a whole new perspective to life.

I look forward to the sounds of birds or pigeons cooing on the prison roof and the clouds drifting into one another just before the summer rain. I can enjoy this as much as seeing the different ties my lawyer wears each time he comes to see me. Just as in another time, I had waited eagerly for Saturday and Sunday nights when I finished work, so I could press Mo's body next to mine, now I wait for evenings to revive in me all the things I have lost. No longer are they in front of me but it does not stop me remembering the anticipation or the swollen easy times we would have together, lying together behind closed shutters.

The thought of the 'roaring crystals' dance just as loud in my life here and make me laugh just as the hallucinatory lows passed across slow Sundays. They paint an imaginary picture of my time at sea or when I hear the waves rolling through Dada's stories. Shabela's sea house with its wooden stilts is a single diversion; a moment of chance like the dance of the pale swallowtail butterfly across our sandy inlets. The life we share up and down the beaches out of the city becomes easy with dreams when I leave the house of my mother and father and all the stuff rocking in my head is eased in the blue spaces of Dada's song. My father's coercive beatings only serve a deeper fear within himself; I know this now.

There are so many people worse off than me. Dada used to say that anyone could get used to anything. He always used to tell me that when he'd got a bad ship or when the engineer turned nasty and called them all

Chink bastards, which he wasn't anyway, and got as much bad stuff from them as he ever did from the white officers, you could always get your own back. If you only stayed quiet and kept your own counsel, things settled down and you settled with them but you did not forget. He'd seen the older ones toiling under the Japanese army on the river during the war and that was no picnic but they'd got on with it. Surviving is everything and swerving at the right moment just as important as the wooden staves they had driven into the septums of the occupying soldiers after 1945.

Most of the early times in here I have not been given much to think about. The first few months pass slowly and the weather is miserable. But I wake up one morning and realise what Dada is telling me is true. I start to think different. During that early time I am obsessed by the idea of sex. It is natural in one so young. Before then I had never given it a thought but now it occupies everything, not just Mo but everyone!!!! They tell me later there are sixty different ways of 'doing it' behind bars. Maybe this is what my father is trying to correct in me.

I start to think of all the ones I've known so they become real to me again, all the men and women I have loved, I can feel their presence beside me, their faces arousing all my wants in this small cell. It upsets me at first but it kills the time. I think if I can do this with my feelings of desire, I can do it for anything, the ships, the sun, the river, my life, my Dada's life, and even those people who are unkind to me with all their grand thoughts of exalted citizens. They all melt slowly into the pot of my imagination.

If you take time step by step it wipes everything away,

moment by moment, seconds, minutes and hours and fills the room with colours and pictures. It makes me laugh, the wealth of it all. This way you can spill your thoughts like gold coin or treasure within your own head, unburdened by choice. I have not even started to construct the manifest, those lightning bridges from my student days to work on the dock or the future as my boss used to say in the dynamics and transportation of fish.

I manage to win over the head guard who accompanies the kitchen boy when he brings my meals. Only the 'specials' get this treatment. He is the one who first talks to me about the need. He tells me that's the first thing that everyone ever complains about, even those who have gone without sex on the outside. I tell him it's the same with me and that I find it unfair to be treated this way. Is there not a way around this?

'But this is exactly why you are in prison.' he says.

I ask him why, it has nothing to do with my crime and he says 'Exactly.' again.

I hadn't thought of it like this before but I have to agree with him.

'It's true,' I say, 'otherwise what else would be the punishment?'

'Now,' he says, 'at least you understand how things are. The others don't and they either find other things to do or it kills them before their time.' He leaves then.

'You'll be all right now.' he calls out from behind the door.

It is the same with the issue of cigarettes. When I first come here to prison, they took away my belt, my shoelaces, my necklace and everything in my pockets including my smokes.

Once inside my cell I ask for them back but they tell me it's not allowed until everything is processed. The first days are really rough. That got to me the most. All day long I kept feeling nauseous and I couldn't understand why they wouldn't let me have something that would do no harm to anyone else. I keep seeing the faces of those two poor white tourists who in truth are not much younger than me with their beautiful shirts and cotton trousers and smart leather running shoes with thick white socks they all seem to wear in Europe. They smell of flowers and silk and linen in the way Europeans do when they are not shouting or being sick.

Their image recedes like the waves and I do not feel the weight of the slap anymore. It has melted into other pictures scattered about my 'room'. It is around then I start to suck on pieces of wood to concentrate. I pull them off the boards of my bunk. Later I understand that the withdrawal of my cigarettes is also a punishment given to me but before I accept that, I already know I have my answer, my tactics in place. Smoking would no longer bother me.

I take hours to shape a splinter from the board until it looks like a matchstick and then I pop it in my mouth and hold it there like the way I used to smoke my cigarettes. Sometimes I would remember the exact moment of the sky when I smoked, or the shape and smell of an oleander tree when sheltering from the rain. Straggly or thin, fat or lumpy pieces of splinter they are all the same to me now.

I shape them, tip them and act tough like in some American gangster movie when I hold them to my mouth. I use the pan as my mirror. They become associated with other images. The absence of cigarette is no longer a punishment to me but instead a pointed reminder of all what my life has been, precious, a gift, a journey never marked by time but time as the present running through me.

Apart from those initial problems nothing makes me too unhappy. Time is always the big master but once I understand that I can do nothing about when it passes through me on its own journey then things become a lot easier. I stop being bored all together when I learn how to remember. It is such a simple thing but you need time to do it. You are never burdened by what you should be doing like you are on the outside.

Sometimes I would start thinking about my room and imagine starting at one end of it and walking around in a circle while listing mentally all the things I passed. In the beginning it took no time at all but each time I started to do it again it would take a little longer. And over time walking around my cell as if it in my own room at the Dada's and then sitting down afterward it always took a little longer than the time before and then even longer because I would remember all the different pieces of furniture, their colour and texture, soft, hard, marks, scratches or chips. And not just my use of this furniture but who had used it before me; whose other footsteps had walked that floor, sat in that chair, and used that bed. It took a great concentration to obtain a complete inventory.

This drains me but then after a while I start on Dada's room, his chair, the dresser, the bed and the clock itself, the clock my Dada used and the one he gave me when he had to go up country to the home, the clock he has with him on every ship. He never used the *shake man* he said. His alarm would always go off in good time. It had been in his family since the white Rajahs had ruled this side of the island and is a present given to his mother at her marriage, one of the few gifts made to her. The Dada keeps it through his own marriage and my mother's early years. The woman in blue tells me she could remember every finger of its face and which part of the numerals she scratched.

I can see him down below on the Blue Funnel boats, going to the harbour ports of China and Australia and Liverpool and the alarm of that clock ringing through every part of him as a marker to his life and to what he had become.

I become such an expert at this that by the end of a few weeks I became a specialist in every part of the house of my Dada. I could spend hours simply listing everything in my bedroom and putting them in a category of order. The more things I thought about, the more they came back to me. Not only the things themselves but the thoughts and feeling attached to them. When Mo first came over and we lay on the rug, listening to the night, not about his body now but how the rug fits the manifest of my room, the thoughts I'd had on my bed.

When Dada takes me in, his daughter, my mother's bedroom becomes mine and now I associate it with all the sounds and feelings that come from there, like the smell of soap or eggs frying in the kitchen at midday and the taste of coffee, tangible as the fabric of chairs. I have always loved coffee. It is part of my inventory.

Stuff I had not noticed before or had forgotten now becomes part of my wider pattern. I realise that a man could live for a hundred years in prison and not get past the front door of his own house if he put his mind to it. If he is older, he could spend a thousand years and not have enough time to list all his memories, how the days stack together in beautiful communion in the joy of everyday life, once you start to separate their folds. In one respect this great advantage makes you think clearer; how I left my studies and those other silent whispers in that crazed household and those other matters of which I don't like to speak when drugs come to settle within me.

It is memory we need, especially us Sea Dayaks. Why does everyone have to speak two languages here? Are we are not allowed to choose. We have to learn the language of our ethnic group. This is determined by our father. In my case it is useless, we are so integrated I have forgotten my Chinese. The Sea Dayaks do not have a specific tongue. They are like rare dirt with their Catholic tastes but they are ignored. And rightly so is how my mother and father view the picture. They need me near to consolidate their truth. I learn like a good student and even throw a little English into the mix for good measure.

'Forty years at sea allows you many tongues,' the Dada says.

Chinese, Malay or Dayak, nobody teaches him to sing. It brings him pain but it is also what makes the Kalimantans put their heads back and laugh and call him 'Uncle Sam'.

Sleep is my beginning. I used to sleep badly at night and not at all during the day. Little by little my nights get better and I could also sleep during the hours of light, particularly after a heavy trawl with all its associated thoughts and feelings, and the life of people passing in and out and through me like dancers waltzing across the floor, the way we danced in clubs.

These acute reminders would tire me and I would sleep but then wake refreshed and start again. It is a case of staging my time after meals and the night winds or the warm sound of the rain to send me dozing off through the day. In the finish sleep claimed between sixteen and eighteen hours a day in preparation for the next bout of memory for which I needed to be fresh. If you throw in the time for eating then my days fold together like the leaves of a concertina.

'Good sleeping weather.' Dada would say when they entered cold waters.

'Your bunk will always keep you warm.'

Apart from visits to the prison yard, I have little time for exercise. Sometimes even visits to the policeman interrogator or my lawyer checking certain facts come as a rude interruption. Six hours to spend with my meals, my basic needs and the story of the man from France is more than enough to entertain me.

Between my mattress and the wooden bed I had found a worn scrap of paper, yellow with age. It had become almost completely stuck to the back of the mattress and the authorities must have thought it a label or description of the make of the material. It is taken from the Sarawak Times but the date is indecipherable, the same as the beginning of the article. A story that must have happened somewhere in France many years before between the mountains and the sea, the paper is yellow and crossed with brown markings at the creases.

A man leaves his poor village in the country north of Marseilles to go down to the sea. He sails away to make his fortune. Twenty-five years later when he returns from America, he is rich. He comes home with his wife and young child. His mother is old now and runs a small Pension there, near to the house where he and his sister have been born and brought up on their small farm. He leaves his wife and son in the other larger hotel and goes to his mother's place to surprise them. The old lady doesn't recognise him when he comes in. As a joke he has the idea of asking for a room. He lets them see his money and cards he carries in his wallet. During the night, his mother and sister enter the bedroom to rob him. They beat him to death with a hammer and throw his body in the river which would carry it away to the sea in the same manner that he had set off to escape his poverty. The water carries him away again like some tragic trilogy. When his wife arrives in the morning, holding her little boy by the hand and not knowing what has happened; she informs the mother and sister of his real identity.

The mother hangs herself and the sister throws herself down a well.

'You keep things from people and that's when the trouble starts,' the lady in blue says.

I read this story a thousand times and try to make sense of it. On the one hand it seems entirely improbable. Who wants to play a trick on their family like that? And then I think it's quite possible when you have something to prove.

Duplication takes place every day. It often comes by chance, the same chance as with my actions that fateful Sunday. In any case I think that traveller sort of got what he deserved. You can never mess around with stuff like that.

When my father tells the Dada out of spite that I know the circumstances of his birth, then they say he starts to get old and sick.

'Sick.' the Dada says and grunts.

'They make me sick what they say about me; sick that I did not tell you more myself. A stain can last forever on this forsaken island. They reduce us Dayaks to an exhausted past. Kill our rich culture in making boats, sailing them, telling stories, all the myths that sustain us, they make disappear.'

My parents think their kind and clever son would disown him like the rest of the family, the politicians and the State. But I am on another journey. Between the hours spent in sleeping and remembering things in all their blonde, red and green patterns I read a French story again and again. Watching the light fade in my cell and grow strong again with the grey fingers of dawn, I travel great distances. Distances as real to me as any life I have lived on the outside. I'd read somewhere that people ended up losing a notion of time in prison and this is what kills them. That is nonsense. Every moment of my life is realised as it ticks through me.

A clarity the size of a cold fish knife held in the crease of my elbow is one that cuts to the bone, not at all like Iskra's little blade used on those two poor lost souls. These are my days. Easy breathing days that become so extended they run into one another. My siesta can be my night's sleep for one day or separates me from another merely by a cat nap in the afternoon. The names of the week became lost but not to my sense of time. Yesterday and tomorrow are not as important to me as the present. It is my fortress.

One day the guard tells me that I have been there for nearly nine months. I believe him but cannot quite understand either. To my mind either nine minutes or nine years could have gone by. The same day plays itself out endlessly in my cell and I set my goals accordingly by the stars like any pirate. Maybe Dada knew it would come to this and taught me in silence from all of his time on the sea, with those chartered voyages taken on tramp ships that ran between islands and crossed the oceans for years on end. He could do his own counting.

The woman in blue could have been the daughter in the story from France, the one who threw herself down the well. It would have fitted with her own sense of sorrow that things never really fit together until they are part of someone else's existence. She gushes out her story to me.

'Not a month after the pirates are captured, and the rebellion put down, many hung, others put in camps, then the Rajah takes your great grandmother. Oh he is a terror, his wife, the Lady fast asleep in their bed of silken sheets, when he has her below. So it continues even after he "put" her with his Chinese manager. He still comes for her whatever the season. Others come and go but he always returns to her, well after the boy is born, always insisting.

'How could your Dada be any different?' she says.

When the guard has gone, I look at my reflection in the metal dish. My face appears grave even when I try to smile. They say this happens when you think a lot. Even if you're happy, you don't look it because you are given over to thought. I remember Saturdays with Mo. I stretch my face out in front of me and try to smile but my features still have the same, harsh frown.

With the days ending, the hours approach that I don't

like to talk about. Fear rises inside me like a stalk, that nameless time when the sounds of the night ring throughout the entire prison and you can hear groans and sighs and other sounds where placation or repentance are called upon. When you come away from drugs, doubt is always printed upon the patina of the soul. Then the sounds fall slowly away, rhythmic as a cortege of silence that dies with the small hours.

I walk over to the little window and tried to study my reflection once again but the light is gone. Instead I can see among the patterns, the same open generous faces that gleam back at me from the dark. Why should it not be like this, an image of those who I have killed? An image contained and serious, my situation is very serious. My features will not lie but I can hear my own voice sound within me.

It chimes like a bell and it rings and rings and says, Dayak, Sea Dayak. Do not deny yourself a thing. You are full of richness and spirit. This voice would serve me as a pirate; a voice strong and resonant, one which normally has passed by me. I am not the accused. I recognise it as the sound that has sunk deep and strong within in me throughout the days of remembrance. It asks for more of me, as if I have been given warning.

Dada is speaking to me on one of my visits to the home upriver. He suddenly sits upright on his bed. He has been lying there as part of his afternoon rest but his eyes are now suddenly bright.

'Take comfort, take comfort my people,' he says, 'your hardship will not last, and neither will you waste away in sadness. Do not let sorrow seize you nor fear that you will not be saved.'

He looks me straight in the eye. 'These are the prayers of every imposter.' he says.

'They put me in jail with those words.' he says. 'Find your own way. We are all strangers to each other even though we sing the same song.'

He once had an Indian lover of Arabic descent. She was very beautiful, an older woman like him but beautiful; more beautiful than any woman I had seen at the house. She wants to write a history of caste and practice and the love of Islam in Malaysia. She says that it runs like a jewel through our history across these islands.

'Not in Sarawak,' my Dada says, 'we are all in the mix here that is why we wear Blue. Those who are high on the fundamentals hate it. Blue is the colour of muddied blood; the blood of the virgin mother, a mix of the underground and the divine.'

The dignified lover looks away and tells the Dada that her book is going to draw a line where Islam has run from the peninsula down to Papua New Guinea and no island of our many thousands has remained untouched by the great wind that rushes out from the desert. Her book would capture the sad role of the woman who brings shame to her family by lying at the feet of the labyrinth; too close to the sun or too near to the sea. The tale reminds me of old Srino's parrot.

'Islam is a beautiful religion,' I hear my Dada say, 'but it is not mine.'

He then tells her of his own history. She does not shudder nor flinch and denounce him as his own family had done but a distance grows between them. We do not see her around much any more which is a shame. I really like her.

'It is not within me to love the beauty of women.' the Dada once tells me before he enters the home.

'I don't know Dada.' I say and look away. I am not comfortable with the confidences the old sometimes share with the young.

Here in my cell, there is no way out unless you breathe and wonder at the interminable silences and the long nights of prison with that voice singing deep within you. Hearing it sound through all the shapes and patterns within you brings a reminder of not only what you have lost but also what you have been given, the greatest gift, the gift of the spirit, where it comes from or where it goes, as deep as any ocean. Will any of the shallow waves that surround our shoreline not encounter this soul of a pirate? I am ready for my trial. My disdain is enough for all.

Chapter Eight

The prison visit

My case is progressing as the police put it. Sometimes when the conversation deals with general matters, they even include me. I continue to breathe like a free man again. During these meetings, no one is unkind to me, everything is so natural, so well organized and so serious that I have the ridiculous impression that unlike my friends on the outside I have become one of the families of the law and we can all be great pals together.

Iskra has been a very good boxer in his day but sadly he busted his knee while out running on the roads. When the physiotherapists see him, he thinks he's in the company of fellow professionals who have come to assess the problem but in reality they are only being nice because the insurance companies dispute his accident claim. It doesn't take him long to find out he's just another client.

'I've learnt everything I know from boxing.' he says.

It's the same with me the law has disabused me of any

fancy notions. I'm just a prisoner getting by, happy to share a joke now and then.

Throughout the entire eleven months of my incarceration it is a surprise to realise that the only times I have ever really enjoyed in company are the rare times when the detective would walk me to the back door, pat me on the shoulder and say to me in a friendly tone of voice, 'That's all for today our little friend.' He sounds like my Dada when he talks of ships and rivers and the Blue Funnel Line. Iskra calls me and Mo 'his little gangsters' but it's not the same. I would have tears in my eyes at such kindness when he passes me back to the guards.

Certain things I never like talking about are now very clear. He has caught me there that old Chinese policeman with his little acts of kindness. He comes close. I realized after my first few days in prison that it wouldn't do to dwell on that part of my life. Mo knows it and that is enough. He doesn't find it so very strange; 'They always have to correct you across this island,' he says 'because they are so uncertain of themselves'.

Too much passes between sex and nation here. This is all news to me; like if someone suddenly asks you if you've had a happy childhood? It's not only the Dada who falls into such huge rages, he could have been a doctor of them, but my father also has his own explosions.

Later, such worrying no longer bothers me, no longer is it necessary to worry or wonder what might happen after Dada's death. To tell the truth prison goes by me after the first few days especially when I master the time thing. It's like being in another place not quite your own but with everything you own all around you.

It's like when the fish dock rages with fire after some-one has set alight a Thai trawler, or you wait for the bell to ring on busy days or when someone chases a drug boat, hoping they get there first before the police. Something is vaguely waiting to happen, to enjoy days as rare as unbroken sunshine that only resolves itself when you let everything pass. Mo tells me they won't let him come to see me because he isn't family. From that day on, I know precisely where I live. This cell has become my home and my life would end here.

The night they arrest me, they lock me up in a room with several other prisoners most of whom are from Kalimantan. They laugh when they see me. They ask what I've done and I say I have killed two white boys with a knife and they all go quiet. But a short time later, they show me how to set up the straw mat where you can sleep. By rolling up one end you can make a sort of pillow like they used to do on a seaman's bunk. They need not have bothered. I know this from the Dada who used to talk about the straw palliasse they had to take down to the ship when he first went away. A don-key's breakfast they call it but I let them show me just the same as a gesture of collective kindness.

Bugs crawl across my face all night long. A few days later they put me in a cell by myself where I sleep on a wooden bed the size of a bunk. I have a bucket for a toilet and a metal washbowl which you could shine and use as a mirror. The prison lies right at the top of the town and I can see the sea through a little win-dow ringed with iron. I am by myself. Iskra must have fixed it. I think I could even catch a glimpse of the outer docks and, if not the water, hear the sounds of ships' engines. Very early in the morning the sounds of the river rise up and with it the beat of the pumps on the fishing boats. I could imagine where my dock lay but I couldn't see that.

One day I am holding onto the bars of the window and straining out. It is hard in the blinding light and better when the clouds come, just before the rain, when the sky dulls over and everything becomes green. A guard comes in and tells me I have a visitor. I pray it would be Mo. I say a silent prayer to Iskra.

To get to the visitors area, you have to walk down a long corridor then up a flight of stairs and finally down another corridor. The prison is like a ship with its sloping decks and alleyways full of shade and brightness. I go down into a very light, very bright room, lit by an enormous window. They have divided it into two sections with two large sets of bars that run down through the middle. Between the two sets of bars is a space of between one or two feet that separates the prisoners from the visitors and a series of high chairs set in a line. Dada has told me about his time here after the strike. Prisoners tell me it hasn't changed much.

I see Mo sitting opposite me, his face is drawn and he wears dark clothes which is unusual for him. My first thought is to indicate why he hasn't worn his striped white suit. He smiles and gives me a little wave.

There are about ten prisoners or so to my side, most of them Indonesians. Mo is surrounded by women and sat between two other visitors perhaps that is why he looks uncomfortable, hemmed in like that. One is a little old Kalimantan woman with pursed lips and dressed all in black and a bareheaded fat woman who shouts everything while making lots of gestures like they do over there. It is the distance between us that makes everyone shout.

The first time I come in, I feel dizzy with all the noise, it is like returning to the fish dock on a Saturday morning when the left over weekend catch is sold and everyone out and the prices being driven down, or the first time I note the faces of the jury. Such a commotion distracts me. I want everything quiet like in my cell or on the day they bury my Dada.

The large bare walls of the room and the sunlight pouring in through the windows makes the difference between the shade of my cell and this place all the stranger. It takes me a second to adjust and then I can see each face clearly outlined against the bright light. I notice two guards sat at each end of the corridor between the bars. Many of the prisoners and their families sit on the floor facing each other. It seems quieter that way. They aren't shouting. In spite of all the commotion they manage to hear each other clearly even though they speak very quickly, almost in whispers but all seemed to join in. The muffle of their voices carries like a calm sea and creates a sort of soft background music against the flow and turmoil of the shouting above. The noise bounces and flows above their heads and echoes from wall to wall.

I pick this up quickly as I walk towards Mo. He is already leaning towards the bars and smiling at me as brightly as he can. He looks very beautiful and sad in his sombre dress but I don't tell him that.

'Well,' he says very softly 'so here we are. Do you have everything that you need?'

'Everything.' I say.

'That's good.' he says.

We fall silent but Mo keeps on smiling. He would look

down and then up at me and our eyes would briefly meet and he would look down again. The fat woman shouts at the man next to me. Her husband is a big, light skinned man with an honest face who could have worked down on the dock there if they let him. She continues a conversation they have already begun some time ago.

'Saba didn't want to take him.' she shouts at the top of her lungs. 'Right,' the man says, 'right.'

'I told her you'd have him back when you got out but she said you wouldn't want to take him because he's not yours.'

The man looks as if he could just sit on the floor and make light, easy stuff, whispering with his hands, like the others.

Mo shouts that Iskra says hello and I reply 'Thanks.' but my voice is blocked out by the man who is asking: 'Is the kid all right or is he fucked up?'

His wife laughs and shouts back and says, 'Never better, he has a job with the *runners* now, the only 'Mantan they'll let near the water.'

Something inside make me shudder and I feel a wild pain of longing for this boy I had never seen. To go swimming where he might go after his running or paint the side of ships or decks who like Dada says he grew up in the sea and that each time there came the sound of a distant siren from a tug, it would always remind him of home bound ships and the longing to be away again. The noise of the docks is to him a form of soothing. He says it reminds him of Liverpool or San Francisco and the great drink and nights he has had gambling and dancing there.

The prisoner on my left is a small young man with delicate hands who never spoke. I notice he is sitting opposite the little old woman in black clothes and that the two of them are staring at each other intently but I do not have time to watch them anymore.

Mo shouts, 'Don't give up.'

'Yes,' I say.

I look at him and want to touch the hair that has streamed out behind him in nights of closed shutters but he has it all tucked away now. He starts to list the contents of food prices and how dear and expensive everything is now and the price of vegetables.

'So many people are taking allotments to supplement their gardens.' he says and then tells me he goes shopping every day.

He does not mention Dada's apartment or how beautiful everything is in the water under the sun or on his shoulder when we were on the beach together, or nights under the window in the rain and the feel of his soft clothes that he doesn't wear now. I don't know exactly what to say. Maybe I should take him away from his vegetables and the cost of food. Surely there must be a code to all this but maybe people don't speak of the thing in question before them; it is always about something else. That must be true because Mo keeps smiling and all I can see are his bright teeth and the little wrinkles around his eyes and think of our time together.

'You'll get out and we'll go to the market again.' he shouts again.

'Do you think so?' I ask, mainly because I have to say something.

Then he says very quickly and very loudly that of course I will be acquitted and we'll be able to go swimming and cups his hand s around an imaginary bowl that might have been a pipe. I remember old Srino's gesture in the room and start to laugh at the double image but I suppose he means a small rice bowl after all. I notice he looks around before he does this. He need not bother because the fat woman continues to shout and no guards come anywhere near. She bawls that she has left a basket of food at the clerk's office and how dear and expensive everything is now because the warehousemen and fisherman had won their rise in wages but what about the ordinary family? Her shouting blocks everything out. Maybe that is a good thing? 'What about the beach? 'I blurt out. Mo shudders.

The young man next to me and his mother are still watching each other like little birds. The murmuring of the Indonesians below us comes like the sound of water that continues to wash our feet. Outside the light seemed to fall intensely against the window. I feel slightly sick and relieved when I see a worm of a cloud appear and know the rain would come soon. Inside, the noise is painful to the ears. I want to stay with Mo and I want to leave this place and I want to hold his eyes as long as I can, losing instead my sense of balance. I don't know how much time passes; Mo tells me about his new life at home and never stops smiling. He is going to shop for lamb's kidneys after he has seen me he says.

I remember Iskra's room but hear my father's words.

'We are a very fair minded but stern country,' his face would change when he makes this statement. His hand would rub my back and I would feel his oiled fingers. I don't remember much about the first time but soon realise the real danger would come later; the soft footfall on the stairs, the putting away of violence and the almost tender touch on the skin.

'I must relieve God's judgement upon you.' he would say.

In the visiting room; the murmuring, the shouting, the conversation continues all around, the only oasis of silence is the small young man and the elderly woman who continue to sit silently looking at each other. Gradually the Kalimantans are led out. Almost everyone stops talking as soon as the first one has left. The little old woman moves closer to the bars just as the guard gestures to her son. He says simply, 'Goodbye Mama.' She slips her hands through the bars and attempts to touch him in a little wave and sad goodbye. She leaves just as a man holding his hands together comes in to take her place. Another prisoner is led in where her son has been and the two men start to talk excitedly. They speak softly enough even though the room has quietened. They come to take away the man to my right and his wife shouts as if she hasn't realised.

'Take good care of yourself,' she bellows. 'we'll be fine.'

Then they come for me, I try to mouth a kiss to Mo but he has turned away.

'Look after yourself.' he says.

He looks up at me and his eyes are full of pain but he doesn't move his face nor crush it against the bars with the same, tense, distressed smile of the little woman. His gestures might have been betrayed by the thoughts raging inside him but I guess it just embarrassed him. Maybe he thought it best not to talk of our good times together or remind me of them.

He writes to me soon afterwards, but he doesn't say anything about himself or Iskra or even the price of food and that seemed to be that.

These are things I do not want to hear anyway. I couldn't really complain because it is easier for me than some of the others in here. I keep thinking of the big Indonesian with the honest face. The guards give the big ones a hard time. They think they are all mixed up in gangs and drugs and the rackets. They give them trouble. How he must have suffered when he came down to greet his fat shouting wife.

The beginning of my imprisonment is the most difficult with the thoughts of a free man; worse, of wanting to sail the boats upriver again to where trade is everything and a Dayak's life is easy. Obsessions come to me of wanting to be away or sailing around one of our tiny islands, with only my men and the palm trees for company. Give me a sudden blast of rock to blow through my veins and the music that I imagine would carry me across the sea and away to the southern Philippines or the pirate's channel of the Moluccas with enough weed to enable me to see everything passing in blue.

Instead all I possess is the safety of the enclosed space. I think of the way Dada on the ships arranges his cabin and bunk and makes a palace of his own confinement with the occasional sprinkle of mementos bought ashore in places like New York and Pernambuco or on the roaring wharfs of Western Australia. It is the stuff that keeps him afloat through the long stretches when he must have wondered where his real home lay...

'Is there anywhere we can call home or do we carry the mattress all our life?' he says.

The woman in blue is speaking to me again. I can see her now.

'Your father is a coward. He hits you when he does not have the courage to say to you what he really needs to say himself.'

I see her pause and chew her lower lip. I recognise the moment. I can see it in myself when confronted by those things I do not like to speak about; the moment when those who never dare, come forward; their thoughts arriving at the breaking of the dam, when the need to say something becomes irresistible. What brings a person to it? Does the Dada dance in her head like he does in mine? Is it fear, grief, anger or just an immense weariness that she feels, the words spilling like coin when she gushes out her stories to me at the beach house?

In this situation I can hear the sounds of the water and little waves that break upon the beach and the need to be near my Dada and the Dayak vagabonds preying upon their unsuspecting victims who step delicately from their ships and trading posts on the coast; the sensation of the river and music playing and the feeling of freedom bring joy to me and the men and women who sail with me. It strikes me now just how much the walls of my prison cell have closed in around me not to contain but to embrace me. The feeling stays. Afterwards, I have only the thoughts of a free man awaiting conviction and adapt myself to the system here.

Chapter Nine

Freedom and incarceration

They interrogate me several times after my initial arrest, but they are just preliminary investigations to establish my identity and don't last long. Iskra has spoken for me but I do not know if money has changed hands. That first time at the police station everyone seems to know of my case but now they act as if they are not interested like they are waiting for the Man.

'It's a Malay thing,' they say.

'We can't afford to be seen as too European.'

A week later however the junior magistrate looks at me with a certain curiosity. To start with he only asks my name and address, my job title, date of birth and the place where I was born. Then he wants to know if I have a lawyer.

I say, 'No, and why the necessity?'

'Why?' he asks.

I reply that I find my case is a very simple one.

He smiles and says, 'That's one way of looking at it, but the law is clear, if you do not have a lawyer, the

State will assign you one and it's better that it comes through us.'

I thought it very convenient that the legal system took responsibility for such details and told him so.

He agrees with me and says 'We are a very modern and progressive democracy. The world outside of this hemisphere all thought we would not be able to achieve this but we proved them wrong. The law is very well thought out here.' He nods his head.

In the beginning, I could not take him seriously. The peninsula pirates would have cut his silver tongue out or been killed in the process. Their law is the old law of the islands; kill or be killed. My mind returns to the beach hut and the time the woman in blue first speaks to me.

'Your Dada is not Chinese.' she says and looks at me carefully.

'But it would not matter if he was Genghis Khan or Deng Tsao Ping the Communist; nor less that he leads the seamen out on strike at the moment of this Nation's independence. His real crime is his blood. How could it be different? A mix of white, Chinese and Dayak is what they cannot stand here. His guilt lies in the chain of his being, his secret, the core of his shame, a mud-died history. They want him to serve as example to all they are not as this incubus of a State lumbers into being.'

Her words pour out in a torrent.

This time it is different. The Chinese detective regards me quietly. He begins the interview in a room with curtains at the windows. A small lamp burns on his desk and shines on the wooden chair where I have to sit while he remains at a little distance in the cool dusk.

The rain beats down on the windows.

I have read of scenes like these in American detective books. It all seems like a game to me. After those other, brief, conversations I study him more carefully, I see a small man, like me, with delicate features and deep blue eyes. There is Chinese in him and perhaps he sees something of it in me. The top positions do not favour them in the civil service and the police; a policy supported by my mother and father. Is this why Dada causes them so much trouble? My father's acts of contrition always follow his floods of abuse.

'Do not provoke your poor father with stories of the Dada,' my mother would say quietly, her voice as sweet and reasonable as possible in that madhouse. I love her very much.

'We will just sit here quietly together,' she would say. Tolerance would fill the room after my beatings, the contrition and then afterwards, his soft footsteps on the stairs.

'We are not here to question your identity.' the detective says.

He has a scalp almost shaved like a Buddhist monk and soft almond skin. He comes across as very reasonable and actually quite kind in spite of the sometime darting eyes or the fact that I have killed two young white men. 'Your identity is not your crime.' he says again. 'In my field of work it is the eyes that tell the story.'

The next day a lawyer comes to see me in the prison. He is short and chubby and looks as if he dines well. His hair is carefully slicked back and in spite of the heat, I am wearing a tee shirt and shorts beneath a short jerkin, he wears a dark suit with a white shirt and blue tie. The tie and the collar look damp, the way his neck folds over them.

He puts the briefcase down on the wooden bed introduces himself as Mr Ramallah and tells me he has studied my file. My case is a tricky one he says but with the right application he's sure we can make the best of it, if I put my trust in him.

I assure him I would and he nods and says that the investigating officers are very reasonable men. I nod in turn and he says, 'Let's get down to business.'

He sits on the bed and explains that that they have obtained certain information about my private life. They note that my Dada has recently died at an old people's home and that I am a user of drugs. They have made enquiries upriver. The prosecution learns that I have appeared very calm on the day of Dada's funeral and have been seen with a boyfriend, the day afterwards. Here, he flutters at his sleeve. He suggests that we are acting in an illicit manner and contrary to the laws of this country even if this is not the substance of the case against me.

'I'm sorry to have to ask you this,' my lawyer says 'but it is very important. And it will be a key argument for the prosecution if I have nothing to counter it with.'

'What do you want me to say?' I ask.

'That you renounce all illicit acts.' he says. 'This will put us in front of them,' he indicates with his fat fingers.

He wants to help me. He asks me if I had been upset that day. Although I find the question surprising, I tell him that I have been furious and he immediately brightens up.

'Because of the circumstances of your grandfather's death?' he asks and I reply 'no, not at all. Death is a part of life. It is the absences and having to travel all that way into the jungle in the heat after nearly sixty hours of work that kills me. The fate of my Dada is not important but of a love almost lost but not quite because something worse replaces it. I hate his obsessions, they make me furious.'

He looks embarrassed, not only for having to ask the question but more for me.

'My beatings are to correct me on the right path of the nation.' I say. Since my father informs me of the secret of Dada's birth this is what my fury is really about;

'Is this when you finish with your studies and go to live with the old man?' he asks.

I nod. I don't analyse my emotions any more, I just put one foot in front of another with each new day. It's not difficult to explain. I swap my books for labour, a free man within the prison of his days. I love Dada very much but that doesn't mean anything now. Every normal person sometimes wishes the people they love would die and the ones they hate even sooner.

When I say that death is just part of life, the lawyer stops me. He seems suddenly disturbed.

'Don't give them that,' he says, 'please don't give them that. They will cut you to ribbons'.

He makes me promise to definitely not say anything like it in court or to the almond face police officer.

'Tell me again why you were furious. I'm here to listen.' he says.

I explain that one of the characteristics of my personality is that physical sensations often get in the way of my emotions. The day of Dada's funeral I had been very tired after all those hours on the dock, nearly sixty of them before the Thursday afternoon when I could get away. Much of what passes on the day of the funeral has gone by me and I had to drink lots of coffee just to keep awake. I would have preferred it if Dada had not died at that time of the week. I could say that but why bother. It is just the sort of talk like you get off the boss. 'Is it only what you want me to say?' I ask.

My lawyer doesn't seem happy with these comments. 'That's not good enough at all.' he says.

His neck seems to go rigid because the dancing wrinkles are suddenly stilled above his collar. He pauses for a moment and then he says,

'Could we say that you are very worried about this strange relationship that has emerged with your Dada and that is why you appeared calm that day but in reality you are raging inside but you keep your emotions tightly under control?'

'You can say it,' I say, 'but it's only half the truth, what you want me to say always is.'

I think that tiredness has me in its grip. When I can be bothered thinking about it, I detest my father and love my mother, what's wrong with that, Freud knew it all along? Because I'm worn out I don't like to talk about such thing s and people know it , where I work , where I live with Dada and when I see him haranguing people from our balcony, constantly aware of the line of seamen outside of the dock gates all those years ago, it makes me sick. If that is all it takes to be traitorous, then half the people of these islands would be in the firing line.

'That's what I feel.' I say.

He looks at me strangely. As if I disgust him with my absences and my sudden spurts of talk. The way of his glance indicates he sees someone before him who doesn't quite 'get it'.

He tells me rather maliciously that in any case the director and staff of the home would be called as prosecution witnesses and things could turn very nasty for me then.

I point out that Dada's funeral has nothing to do with this other business but he flares up and says, 'That's where you're wrong. You have had only minor dealings with the police and judicial system here. They will twist anything to get a grip.'

I try to remember what the little woman in blue has said to me.

'Your Dada has done his penance.' she says.

'I know he is one of the old Rajah's illegitimate sons.' I say. 'That secret has been laid out before me.'

'As you say but it's not your secret now.' she says.

'There is much wickedness on this island. Your great grandmother was no halfwit but a cheerful girl and merry as could be; a woman of fifteen when the sea Dayaks rose up. When he puts them down, the new Rajah takes her to work in the house but it is not long before he has her beneath him. Nine months later you can see the result. She has become one of the mixes so they couldn't give her back. They got the Chinese to marry her, to look after her and the baby.

'Blood is thicker than water?' I say.

She says, 'Don't you believe it, a baby passed over is a child lost.'

'Your Dada is no more Chinese than anyone, that's why they hate him on the ships and treat him like shit. His blood is the same as all over this scabrous island, maybe that was why he won the seamen over, why they followed him, because of that. All blood is mixed below deck.'

I picture the Dada in full flow from our balcony, a hero to his followers.

'It is never about those working men; more's the pity,' she says.

I remember how the Dada would bellow and rage and beat his chest and I would have to go and calm him before the detectives would arrive once more to our door. Much wickedness on this island, I become quiet and pause for a moment.

My lawyer thinks I have been ignoring him. He leaves looking angry. At one point I am about to call him back and tell him maybe I have been mistaken in my responses but in the finish I don't bother. I don't need him as a friend; I have friends of my own. I don't want his sympathy either, so he can defend me better. Maybe he needs to feel that way if I have made him uncomfortable. I don't want to do that but if he wants to act as if he is a friend of mine, like the ones I smoke, he has to listen to what I have to say. When everything is said and done, he could never be. There is little point in him pretending. And anyway what does he know of life inside. He has never opened a pay packet in his life; even if they are guilty, people like him can always buy themselves out of trouble. The door slams after him.

The next morning is hazy with sun and rain, pewter coloured clouds and a yellow light that streams through the cell. A little while later they take me once again to be questioned by the detective but it is nearly two o'clock in the afternoon before they issue me into the interview room. This time the office is flushed with a different light before the rains of the summer monsoon as if the detective has deliberately changed the atmosphere.

'It is like our history the way it switches across this island.' he says.

The room is very hot. The detective wipes away at his forehead and his face has lost some of its almond calm. He very politely tells me to sit down and says my lawyer could not be there due to unforeseen circumstances. I have a right to not answer any of his questions but I say that doesn't bother me. I can answer anything he wants on my own.

He nods and presses a buzzer on his desk. A young clerk comes in, Malay, and sits down very close behind me. I can picture him shopping on Sunday with his wife, maybe they would come down to the fish market to purchase their weekend merodowsal or special dish anniversary. Maybe they would have children with them, laughing amongst the river crowds. I could not see him as a pirate, with his mortgage and little car and happiness spread all around him.

We both, the policeman and I sit back in our chairs and the interrogation begins. I can feel the Malay's breath against my neck but I ignore it, just like my lawyer's collar of fat. It must be easy and yet very hard to be suburban, knowing everyone is watching you for a slip like my father thought everyone regarded him and so he made my life a curfew. Maybe it is only my way of thinking but that doesn't mean it's not of relevance. I have the Dada to thank for getting me out of that mess. The first thing the detective says to me is that I am depicted as a taciturn and uncommunicative young man and he wants to know what my reaction is to that. I reply that there isn't much to say and that's about it, so I generally keep quiet. He smiles as he had done that first time and I see calmness in his eyes.

'Sometimes that's best,' he says, and then he adds, 'in any case it's of little importance.'

He falls silent, then looks up at me, and says very quickly;

'What interests me is you! There are certain things about you that I cannot comprehend.'

He says he's sure I would help him understand.

'Remember the eyes,' he says, 'they tell me more than you can ever say.'

I recount once again the simplicity of the day. He encourages me to continue ,from what has happened with the woman in blue on the wooden stairs to the hot sand of the beach , the journey back to the city in the rain, the club, the drugs wearing thin when we are descending like parachutes and running from our demons, the terror not yet with me.

'What happens then is just a roll of the dice, I say.

'Does the fight start then, among the light, the darkness, the loud voices, when all you want is a little peace after your long voyage?' he asks.

'Is that how it starts? Do you have a glimpse of the far horizon from your pirate ship?'

After every statement he would say, good, hum, good, hum, like a prayer. When I got to the part where the two bodies are laid out before me on the floor, he nods in approval at the narrative flow. He puts down his pen and says, 'So that's it?'

I nod, suddenly weary of telling the same story, over and over again. It feels like I have never talked so much. Even the markets with the shouting and roaring all day does not make my voice or my head feel as swollen and fatigued as this.

He stands up. There comes a moment's silence. The

policeman says he wants to help me, he really does. He finds me interesting and with God's blessing he can do something for me.

I look up sharply. Does he know Iskra or Shabela?

First he wants to ask me a few more questions. Without pause, he asks me if I ever really love Dada or is it just his influence over me at a time when I am vulnerable.

I say, 'Yes, of course, just like everyone else.'

The clerk must have made a mistake at that moment because he mutters and sighs and has to go back to his original place in the transcript. He must have eaten early because I can smell onion on his breath.

After his corrections a period of quiet take place before we carry on. For no apparent reason, the detective asks me why I keep on using the knife even when both bodies lay motionless before me. I think about this and explain that I used the knife only once; the rest is just a chain reaction like when you cut off a fish's head, the body still wriggles until the nerves die. My reaction is the same except I have the knife in my hand. He does not seem interested.

'Why did you not wait between the second and third time you used the weapon?' he asks. I can feel his eyes upon me.

I want to tell him that I had been breathless and that in catching the second man, the knife became part of the same moment as though it has a life of its own. I don't stand to catch my breath or wait calmly then proceed to stab the young tourist. I can see it now as a film, the beach, the rain, the music, the night, the little explosions inside me joining together in a fusion with the darkness and the shouting, then the slap, the lightning slap that sends me spinning through our history.

But I keep silent. I make no statement nor offer any opinion during this break. The pressure of the day after the flooding of light and the waiting keeps my tongue still. You can feel the clouds gather on the skyline and begin to come lower over the trees but I still remain quiet, serene even in that hot little room.

'Why did you stab a man who was already dead?' he asks again, his eyes never leaving my face.

I don't know what to say. The policeman wipes his forehead and repeats the question in a slightly quieter tone.

'Why? I must insist you tell me, why?'

I remain silent and feel the slight breeze; it is always like this before the rain.

He stands suddenly and goes to his desk at the other end of the room. He opens a drawer and rustles around inside it. Has he gone for the knife that the prison guards tell me would be covered in a cellophane plastic to keep the evidence free from contamination? Instead he takes out a set of holy beads and brandishes them in front of me as he comes closer to the desk. In a different voice, the notes almost aquiver, he asks; 'Do you know what these are?'

'Yes of course.' I say.

Before I can finish, he raises his voice. 'These beads are the symbols of the faith of all the religions that have crossed this island.'

He tells me quickly and quietly that he believes in the great and worshipful Buddha, the Christ and the Prophet Mohammed and he is positive that no man, no matter what his source cannot ask nor seek forgiveness from one of these;

'But in order for that release , a man must repent, must bow his head and become once more like a child whose soul is laid bare. He must prepare himself to accept the judgements of the world.'

His entire body leans towards me over the table. The beads are almost directly above me, they smell of sandalwood and the colour of the day. I see the lights in the waterfront club, the ring on the boy's finger, the hand spinning through the darkness like a disco ball and each part of my being slowly being peeled away.

Behind me, in a great silence of anticipation or fear I sense that the clerk has seen this show before. His presence is like a wall behind me. The policeman is holding the beads above me like a child holds a necklace in a game with a prostrate grandfather. His almond face is no longer calm. He asks if I have anything to say, anything different to his accusation.

'Remember we are not here to question your identity.' he says.

I feel hot and yet a shiver of cold runs through me as it always does with the coming rain. I remember the walk behind Dada's coffin when so many thoughts jumble inside my head. There are dusty files hugging the walls of his office and a fly circles above me in the heat. With the beads dangling and clacking together and his incessant voice, I was beginning to lose a sense of coherence. The detective starts to scare me. The machine behind me has ceased to register and even the whirr of the fans seems listless and dull. This is ridiculous. I am the criminal, the accused, not an appellant at a confession.

Just as the policeman seems to sink into his own silence, his voice rises again like a noisy yellow warbler and the beads rattle and clack above me. He simply cannot understand why I have not paused with the knife not once but twice. It is useless to repeat to him again, that I have been wound up, then out of breath, then affronted in the second boy getting away, then confused and hallucinating and furious at the slap that invades me like a crushing wave, an ominous swell that flows between these island and reaches out for me like I have been chosen. They say no wave ever returns to its source but this one enters my life centre.

I ask doesn't he think it wrong to keep pursuing me about this, that he has the facts and the prisoner before him even if I feel a free man. How can he punish me in terms of feelings. Feelings simply aren't important.

'Stop,' he says, 'your case is never about what just happened.'

He draws himself up to his full height. He demands that I believe and if I believe, I will be saved.

'Do you believe?' he asks. I nod to keep him quiet. The hammer might appear from his desk and I do not want that on my fingertips. The Malaysian police retain their humour for only so long.

'Even those who turn away still believe.' he says.

'It is within the core of your being.' he says.

It is his firm belief that if he directs his anger at anyone, it is to help and release them. If anyone says different in such situations they would be lost and his own life would have no meaning. It would have no meaning because he would not have tried sufficiently to understand them.

'Do you want my life to have no meaning?' he shouts.

I hear the clerk shift and shuffle behind me. I say that in my opinion, it is none of my business what gives him meaning. From across the table, the detective launches himself at me, the beads waving in front of him, screaming like a madman, his small oval face drawn down in a paroxysm of rage and anger of someone possessed. Where is the calm and almond countenance of our first experience? I turn to the clerk but his face is also down as if the keyboard is his holy book and should give him no reason to look up.

'How can you not believe that they suffered for you?' the policeman seems to be addressing my entire being.

About to say that I had suffered enough for someone else's beliefs I thought it best to stay quiet. An image of my father rises before me and I think what trouble he might still bring to complicate matters further. After my initial shiver, the room remains still very hot; soon the pavements will be steaming. This is my time. Always whenever I want to get rid of people my head drops, my face turns away and I nod in agreement. To my surprise the policeman stops shouting. He drops everything and his eyes return to quiet as if his thoughts are also closing down, drifting away like a junk or sampan suddenly released from a sunlit harbour.

There is a confidence in his voice.

'You see?' he says. 'You see?'

'You will put your trust in those who suffer for you.' His eyes brim with tears.

Head bowed, I nod again. The detective sits back in his chair; the sweat runs away off his face in small rivulets from his forehead to the delta of his cheeks.

He looks very tired. He sits there in the silence of the moment and gathers his jacket around him, while the clerk, finishing off, completes his work in silence.

The detective looks at me intently and with a little sadness,

'I have never met anyone with such a hardened attitude as you.' he says softly.

'Every criminal who has stood before me has ultimately recanted their sins when faced with such symbols of suffering.'

I had been about to say but they are criminals when I realise I had also joined that club. It is still difficult to come to terms with when you believe yourself free. I have only tried to live my life. The policeman stands as if to indicate the end of the interview.

He asks me then in a slightly weary tone if I regret what I have done. I think about this and rather than go over the whole ground again I ask him if he does not ever feel like being someone else? Could he not live a different life? Are not his ancestors the first traders in accordance with the same history of these islands, before the silver thread of the Rajah's law becomes sacrosanct? He looks a little like the lawyer. As if I don't quite understand, as if before him stands someone totally beyond him. He shakes his head.

'Life is full of regrets.' I say.

Nothing more happens that day.

In the week that follows my arrest I try to interpret the gush of words from the woman in blue. How does she know my mother? Each time I try all I can see is a picture of Iskra slapping his woman or Mo letting his long hair down or changing his shirt, his proud chest thrust towards the window and the sea.

Her story nags at me. But if Dada can defy all the rulers and Tuns and Sultans on this blighted island who am I to give up? The seamen's strike may have brought together all the resentments of those who want control here but the Dada must have seen how it would end. Why does he carry on peddling the same dream? Why so much that it becomes part of him if there is not something else to sustain him when everything appears lost?

During the days that follow I often see the detective in his office. On each occasion my lawyer attends with me and we have no more trickery with the beads. Questions are limited to examining certain points made in my previous statements. Sometimes the policeman discusses the charges with my lawyer but to tell the truth they don't take much notice of me. They see my case as more or less done with but they cannot confine a free man. Nothing happens without a cause and I am the last to break.

No one asks me about Allah or God or Buddha and I never see the detective get as worked up as on that day. As a result our meetings become more cordial. After a few questions and a bit of discussion, the interrogations come to an end. I would return to my cell and they would go to their homes in the suburbs. My mother loves me.

Chapter Ten

Dada's funeral

When Dada dies I receive a telegram from the Home.
It is in the country district upriver. My mother and father
would not go to the funeral. He despises him in life and
there is no difference at his death. My mother stays at
his side.
'I will not be hypocritical.' my father says.
His note finishes, 'very sincerely yours.'
It might have come from another world, the world he
inhabits, rather than a death in a family. A full half century since Dada's traitorous act is nothing to him. They
would not attend his funeral because my father fears
the stain would remain forever.
'He brings shame upon us all, even in death' he says.
The old people's home is like its name, 'The Far Star',
eighty kilometres from Kuching. I could get the bus at
two o'clock and arrive up there for the evening, stay
for the wake and the burial and then set off back to the
City the following afternoon.
That way I could attend and still please the Boss. He'll

no doubt say something when he sees me in the full blue suit. I'd be gone a couple of nights. He wouldn't know I'd be back home by tomorrow night. That way I can also wrangle a little time extra for myself like any Dayak or pirate would do. I ask my boss for two and a half days off. He can't say no given the circumstances but I take three and a half including the weekend. He doesn't seem happy.

I even say to him: 'It's not my fault.' But he doesn't reply.

Then I think why do I have to say that? I have nothing to apologise for. He is the one who should have been offering me condolences.

For now, it's as if Dada is not dead. After the funeral, however, it will be over and done with and the matter officially closed. I will get the bus at two o'clock. It is very hot.

I feel a little strange because I have to go up to Jamila's place to borrow a black tie. I also ask for a piece of red cloth to tuck in my sleeve. She lost her uncle a few months ago.

I ate in silence at the restaurant as I always do. Everyone feels very sorry for me, and Jalima says:

'You only have one Dada.' When I get up to leave, they walk me to the door; there is no sign of the little woman in blue.

Dada's resting place is a modern country institute with a set of individual 'cottages' built around its perimeter. All of the dwellings are daubed in white or yellow, green or red like the different kampongs around our city district and the same as the houses on the ridge at the beach.

'Community is very important here as with all our customs,' the director tells me.

Ha ha. Poor old Dada has gone back 'home'; an old man, a conduit between the sea Dayaks the island rulers and the Chinese middlemen. Conceived on a couch but never between the silk sheets of the governors 'French' house, he breaks all their rules.

'Who would have my provenance?' he asks.

A bastard son passed over to one of the Chinese managers who poses as his step dad and gets him away on the ships of the Ocean Steamship Company as soon as he's old enough. He stays there more than twenty years, out of sight, until the seamen's strike.

'The sea absolves you of everything.' he says.

After I had collected my various pieces of clothing, I run to catch the bus. Rushing around, running like that, plus the bumpy ride and the smell of petrol and the sun's glare reflecting off the road and all that is behind me, in my haste to get away, makes me drowsy when I sit down. I sleep for nearly the whole journey. When I wake up I am leaning against a market woman who smiles at me and asks if I have come a long way. I said 'Yes.' so I wouldn't have to talk anymore.

The home is not directly at the centre of the village. I walk. I don't want to think about Dada right away. There are things you should just leave aside. Even as a child I would hear my father say how the Dada brought disgrace to us all and my mother would start to cry.

'We are the unfortunates of our kampong.' she wailed. I can remember my face around the door. My father tells me that Dada is a bad man and I am not to talk of him. I nod. He says Dada has a 'Chinese character with a Dayak soul and that is not good for Malaysia or the Malays.'

'Why can't we honour him?' I ask my mother. 'They teach veneration and respect at school.'

My father must have heard. She might have told him. She swears she didn't. The old man instructs me to go upstairs and lie on my bed. He follows me and takes off his rattan belt and that is where another episode in my life begins.

The care nurse informs me I have to meet the doctor first. He is busy at present. I have to wait a while. The nurse talks the whole time. She is from North Kalimantan, the poorest part of the Old Dutch districts. Then I meet the director.

He shows me into his office. He has the Chinese doctor with him. He is a short elderly man, who wears the legion of Independence pinned to his jacket. The director looks at me closely with his pale blue eyes, I thought a little strangely. Then he shakes my hand. He holds onto it for so long that I don't quite know how to pull it away. He glances at some papers, and then says: 'Your grandfather came to us some time ago. You are the only one who would support him financially then.'

I think his face has turned reproachful for something and I start to explain about my mother and father and Dada. But he stops me.

'You have no reason to justify yourself. I've read your Dada's file. You are able to look after most of his needs but later he requires a nurse. You earn a very modest living. And to tell the truth, he is happier here with us. His seaman's pension keeps him comfortable.'

The unspoken question of my parent's absence hangs in the air. The director does not ask why this is a Chinese funeral, a Catholic funeral like those that takes place in the ports of southern China, or Singapore at the bottom of the peninsula whose name *Si* we still include within our name even though they have absented themselves from the Federation because of the bigotry.

I agree and say: 'Yes, Governor.' The Chinese doctor remarks quietly that the Dada has good friends here.

'You know;' he adds, 'people of his own age love him. He can share his interests of the past with them. You are young and he probably has got bored living with you.'

It's true, the latter days, when we live together, Dada increasingly spends all his time in silence. He would finger the lapels of his collar watching people come and go and sometimes hug his arms around him. He looks at me with an increased gaze but he doesn't say much.

When I go to live with him he knows I know of the secret of his birth. My father in his bitterness has told me to drive me away from him but the opposite happens. I love him more. He still shouts down to people but less now, nor does he get excited in the way that once inflamed him. He is becoming tired. The first few days at the old people's home, they tell me he often cried. But this because of a change to his routine rather than any pain; my mother and father would never come to see him and most of my time is now spent working on the dock.

After a few months at the place, he comes to call it his home. He would have cried if he'd been taken or moved away for the same reason. It is partly why I had gone to visit him as much as I could during his early time there. I have been less and less this past year. It takes up my whole Sunday not to mention the time and effort to buy the ticket, to catch the bus and travel more than two hours each way. It was worth it at the time when he first went in but then my own life starts to change and I need some space. The empty apartment rooms can bring their own solace.

The director is talking to me again but I'm barely listening.

Then he says: 'I assume you would like to see your Dada.'

I stand up without saying anything and follow him out the door. On the staircase, he explains: 'We put him in our little mortuary so we don't upset the others. Every time one of our residents passes away they feel anxious for two or three days. It makes it difficult for us to do our job when there is so much emotion about.'

We walk through a courtyard where there are a lot of old people chatting in little groups beneath the trees. They stop talking as we walk by. Once we had passed, their conversations start up again. They sound like small sea birds calling in the distance and Old Srino's predicament comes back to me. When we reach the door of a small building, the director stops:

'I'll leave you here, Mr Rana Abdullah. I'll be in my office if you need anything.' He pauses to go and then looks at me strangely again as if he wants to say something. 'The funeral is set for ten o'clock tomorrow morning so you can attend the wake of your dearly departed tonight. One more thing: your Dada, it seems, often told his companions that he wishes to have a Chinese burial but in a particular Catholic style.'

'That's Dada.' I say.

Maybe he has thrown that last bit in for good measure just to make sure everyone knows he's different. Is this really to seek his last rites?

'I have taken the liberty to arrange everything. But I wanted to let you know this.' the director says.

I thank him. While never professing to be an atheist, Dada has never once in his life given much thought to all that religious stuff. He is too busy with his new girlfriends, not to mention his beer and brandy and rum and his resting days with his buddies after the solidarity of the sea.

'The Buddha is within us all.' he used to say and laugh. I go inside. The room is very bright, whitewashed, with a glass roof. There are chairs and trestles in the shape of an X in the centre of the room. Two cross ply frames made of light coloured wood support the coffin and the tip points a particular way towards the big windows. They have already closed the lid. All you can see are its shiny metal screws, barely secured, sticking out from the stained walnut planks. An Indonesian nurse in a white smock, wearing a brightly coloured scarf over her head remains near the coffin.

At that moment, the caretaker comes in behind me. He must have been running. He stammers a little as he speaks:

'We closed the casket, so I have to unscrew the lid for you to see him.'

He starts to walk towards the coffin but I stop him with my hand.

'Don't you want to?' he asks.

'No. He's here inside me.' I reply and point to my heart. He stops and I feel uncomfortable because maybe I shouldn't have said that. Maybe there is a responsibility that you have to view the body. After a moment, he looks at me and asks:

'Why?' but without sounding reproachful, just as if he's simply asking a question.

I say: 'I don't know.'

Then he twirls his grey moustaches through his fingers, and without looking at me, 'I understand.' he says.

He keeps looking at my face as if to see something there, a little like the director, to check if I was really Malay. Not as delicate as the director, Dada would have laughed.

Even though the caretaker is old, he has beautiful bright blue eyes and his face is an even brown with deep creases below his distinguished grey hair. He brings a chair over for me and then sits down himself a little behind me. The nurse stands up and heads for the door. The way her hair bobs under her headscarf makes me feel strange and I realise it is like my mother's, the way she wore hers, red and white striped cotton and a bulge of shining silk tied behind her neck.

Seeing my eyes at that moment, the caretaker says: 'She has a big family.' I don't quite understand what he means, so I look up at the nurse and see that she has a bruise around her cheek bone just below her eyes. It sits a flat blue like an island under some depressed skin that acts like a sandbar away from the side of her face. From where she has been sitting, all you can see is the raised skin around the mark as she stands to go. It makes me think of Iskra's mistress and the way he beat her; the way they beat all women on this island, wives, mistresses, lovers or whores.

'She has to work with you.' the caretaker says.

After the nurse has gone, he says: 'I'll leave you alone now.'

I don't know what gesture to make but he stands at

the back of my chair and doesn't move. His presence behind me makes me feel uncomfortable in the late afternoon with the whole room bathed in a beautiful light. 'We have reached the mountain.' I close my eyes.

It has been a typical day, hot and humid with a sky shot through with sun and a misty visibility that always looked to be clearing. I spot the butterflies, flying outside all around the yard and the early click of the cicadas as an early soundtrack to the evening fall. Amongst the pine trees and rhododendrons, white and mauve cat's whiskers are flowering in the increasing gloom of the landscaped patches that have been cultivated by the home's residents outside their 'homes'. They call them their allotments. Pink Scaripia grows in bushes everywhere.

The tops of the trees are wired through with lightning conductors, a reminder of the ferocity of the thunderstorms, you can get out here. When it comes down even operating a mobile phone is risky. Two flowered Malaysian red admirals weave around the window, their tipped yellow and black wings hover and open like delicate flowers. Darkness soon falls like fire down the barrel of a gun. A gunshot is all it takes here between night and day.

'We have no dusk,' I once heard my Dada say. 'everything here is either one thing or another, life or death.'

'Have you been at this place long?' I ask over my shoulder.

The caretaker immediately replies: 'Five years.' – as if he has been waiting forever for me to speak. Then he talks for a long time. He would have been very surprised if anyone had told him he'd end up a caretaker in an old people's home in this district he says.

'But it's just the way things happen,' he shrugs.

He is seventy four years old and from Kuala Lumpur. I interrupt him to ask: 'Ah, so you're not from around here?' Then I remember that before taking me to the director's office, he has talked about Dada. He tells me they would have to bury him very quickly but not as quickly as the Muslims because it is so hot in the open country, and especially on a hillside where he could see the water. Three days is the maximum they could keep him but in southern China he realises that is only for the poor. They sometimes keep them ten days there. That's a real wake. He looks at me as if he has said too much. Then he tells me what he loves about our capital city.

'I find it difficult to forget it, he says.

'Back there it is so green and people stay with the ill and dying a long time because they know that for as long as they are breathing they can still be with them. The tree line comes right down through the city to the water and brings a sense of peace to everything. Twenty four hours after they have passed away they have to be buried and gone. There is no hanging around like some who never leave the side of the coffin, no time for that, you've barely come to terms with what's happened when you have to rush out to bury them. Here by the sea it's more relaxed but in the interior it is very different.'

'They can't wait to get rid of you.' he says.

His wife bustles in. 'Do be quiet, you shouldn't be telling the young man such things.' She stares at me.

The old man bows his head and apologises. 'It's all right,' I cut in, 'it's all right.' I agree with what he says and find it interesting to note the difference between different customs.

'What is there to hate in that?' I say and think of the history of the Dayaks.

In the little mortuary, the caretaker tells me he has no money at all when he first came to the home. The job pays for his coffee and cigarettes and some little trips he adds.

'Your Dada made me laugh,' he says, 'with his stories, that one about being sewn up in a canvas bag and thrown into a lifeboat and threatened to be lowered away or beaten with hot shovels when the Chinese stokers got drunk on rice wine. He laughed every afternoon when I brought him his secret little drink he shares with Kim Song.'

'This place has been good to me,' he indicates by rubbing his thumb and finger together, 'the little tips that come with certain conveniences.'

Since he considers himself healthy when he arrives at the home, he offers to take on the job of caretaker and that brought him a small wage and even a trip to Kuching now and then, when he and his wife could be bothered to take the bus. I point out to him that when everything is taken into consideration, he is still one of the residents but he denies it flat out and shakes his beautiful head. I had already been struck by the way he says 'they', 'the others' and, more rarely, 'the old people' when he speaks about the occupants, some of whom were the same age as him and some even younger but he doesn't see himself as one of them.

'My wife originally comes from this island and that is why we came back.' he says.

I thought that's why most people come back – because of some decision made outside of their daily lives. I remember my father's footstep on the stairs and knew what was coming. Gradually I realise what starts out as a story of ordinary chance often becomes part of a normal habit, no matter how strange.

'Naturally each case is different.' he says. He is the caretaker and to a certain extent he has more privileges and some authority over the others. Then the nurse comes back in. Night has come suddenly and very quickly, the sky has grown heavy and dark above the glass roof. The caretaker switches on the lights and I became nearly blinded by the sudden burst of brightness. He invites me to come to the dining hall to eat, but I couldn't eat.

He then offers to bring me a cup of coffee. I like coffee, so I say yes, and a moment later he comes back carrying a tray. I drink it. The taste is bitter and good and suits my mood.

'My wife makes it,' he says, 'she likes it strong.'

I want a cigarette. I hesitate because I don't know if I should smoke there in front of Dada. I thought about it: but it is of no importance now whatsoever. Dada would have offered me a drink of brandy if the tables were turned. I could imagine him sitting up in the coffin while everyone around him screamed. I offered the caretaker one. He takes one carefully and we both smoke.

'You know;' he says to me after a moment, 'your Dada's friends are going to come to the wake as well. Even if it isn't the custom for most of them, they still want to come.' He gestures around the room.

'I have to go and get some more chairs and coffee.'

I ask him if he can switch off one of the lights. It is still only the early evening but their harsh reflection off the white walls have the effect of making me feel nauseous. He says it's not possible.

'That's how they work,' he says, 'on or off.'

'Like day and night, all or nothing. Life or death.' He echoes Dada's sentiments.

I don't pay much attention to him after that. I know by his expressions that Dada has brought him into his stories. He goes out, comes back then sets up the chairs. He put some cups around a coffee pot on one of them. Then he sits down opposite me, on the other side of Dada. The nurse takes her place also at the back, but turns away from me so that I can't see what she is doing. Judging by the way her arms move though, I can tell she must be knitting; probably for her family in the north. They have big families across the border. It has become cooler now. The coffee has warmed me and the night air drifts in through the open door, bringing with it the sweet scent of flowers. I think I fall asleep for a while but suddenly come awake by something brushing against me.

My eyes have closed and open now the room seems even more dazzling white. There is not a single shadow and every object, every angle; every curve stands out so sharply that it hurts my eyes. At that very moment, Dada's friends come in. There are about ten of them in all and they silently slip into the room beneath the lights that are blinding me. They sit down and not a single chair creaks.

I look at them as I have never looked at anyone before. I take in every detail of their faces and clothing. But I cannot hear them, so I find it difficult to believe they are real. Almost all the women wear silk sarongs tied tightly around their waists, which make their stomachs look even rounder. I had never noticed how old women can have such big stomachs. They seem to carry them along as if all of their being resides there.

The men are almost all very thin and walk with the help of sticks or canes. The Chinese men walk low on their feet as if they too, like Dada, have spent their lives in the engine rooms of the Blue Funnel Line. What strikes me most about their faces is that I can barely see their eyes, just a faint, dull light in a nest of wrinkles either Chinese or Malay or even one of the Sea Dayaks who looks as lost and full of thought as the rest of them.

Once they sit down their clothes become indistinguishable. Most of them look at me and nod as if they feel embarrassed by my youth. Their lips are sucked in because they have no teeth; I cannot tell whether they acknowledge me or if their mouths twitch involuntarily. I think they are probably acknowledging me. They all sit opposite me, around the caretaker, nodding their heads. For a split second, I have the ridiculous feeling that they are a tribunal sent here to judge me.

Soon afterwards, one of the women starts to cry. She sits in the second row, hidden by one of her friends, and I couldn't really see her. She cries softly, continually; I feel she would never stop. The others don't seem to hear her. They are huddled in their chairs, sad and silent. They look at the coffin or at their canes or some other object in the room. They seem to see nothing else as if their thoughts are already contained in some other compartment of their lives.

The woman keeps on crying. I am surprised because I don't know her. I want her to stop but don't dare tell her. The caretaker leans over and says something but she just shakes her head, mumbles out loud and continues sniffing with the same regular rhythm. My mother once told me that many people have cried for Dada, especially women. But she says it with such disgust and through pursed lips as if she has eaten something sour.

'Some cry for him all their lives.' she said.

Then the caretaker comes over and sits down beside me. After a long time and without looking at me, he explains: 'She was very close to your Dada. She says that he is her only friend here and that now she has no one.' We sit like this for a long time. The woman's sighs and sobs grew fainter and fainter but her snuffles still pierce the silence.

Finally, she falls silent. Not sleepy any more but still tired my back aches. At that moment, the stillness of all those around me becomes hardest to bear. Every now and then, I hear a strange sound as if from outside but I can't make out from where it's from. In the end I realise that some of the old people are sucking in their cheeks, making odd clicking noises. They are so engrossed in their own thoughts that they do not realise they are doing it. I even have the impression that this dead man stretched out in front of them means nothing to them except in that they are rehearsing their own passing, but I could have been wrong about that.

The caretaker serves everyone coffee. I don't know what happens next. The night passes. I remember that I open my eyes at one point and see that some of the old people are asleep, huddled up against each other, except for one man who has his chin resting on his hands his elbows tucked into the side of his stomach just below his ribs. He has no need of a walking stick but still looks frail. He stares at me as if he is waiting for me to fully awaken. He looks Chinese; his glare is like an eagle's. I go back to sleep and only wake up because my back is hurting more and the pain is creeping up towards my shoulders. Dada used to say I should meditate more but no amount of freeing my mind that night could rid me of bad thoughts.

A grey coolness comes in through the glass roof as dawn arrives. A little while afterwards, one of the old people wakes up and coughs a great deal. He spits into a large chequered handkerchief and each time it sounds as if the cough had been wrenched from his ribs, like from behind a watertight door. I think of a trawler below the bow where the Thai smugglers keep the immigrant women. The coughing wakes the others and the caretaker calls the time to go. They have completed the wake he says and should be proud. Everyone stands up. The night has turned all our faces ashen.

To my great astonishment, they each shake hands with me as they file out – as if this time has sealed a bond of intimacy between us, even though we have not exchanged a single word.

Worn out, the caretaker takes me to his room and says I can freshen up a bit. I take another coffee; this time with milk.

'My wife makes it well with or without.' he says.

The coffee is hot and very good. By the time I go outside, the day has fully dawned. Reddish streaks fill the sky high over the hills that separate Sarawak from Sabah. From the sea, the wind has blown in from that direction and carries with it the scent of salt. It looks like a beautiful day before the rain. It has been a long time since I'd been to the countryside and I thought how nice it would be to go for a long walk, if it hadn't

been for Dada. I stand waiting in the courtyard, beneath a tree that is shattered by spears of golden light.
A light, he used to say, that is constant in Australia
throughout November.

I breathe in the scent of the cool earth and don't feel
sleepy anymore. I think about my colleagues at work.
They'd be getting to the market about now. This is always the busiest time of the day with the boats arriving
full of fish that have waited all night in the river. Iskra
would be waking as well but it would be for something
else. Then I become distracted by the sound of a bell
ringing from somewhere inside the home just like you
hear on the quayside before everywhere gets set to
open and the market explodes into life. Here you can
hear the early hustle and bustle behind the office windows and then everything goes quiet as if they realise
what day it is.

I look up. I suppose that's when I started to look at the
sky from my father's house – face down towards the
foot of the bed. Neck craned as if I could see the colours through the window and not feel the lash imprint-
ing against my shirt. The beatings are not the worst.
The footsteps on the stairs come later, always after the
dark, when an air of eternity would close around me
and the light get sucked into a kind of simple silence
before the door opens gently and my father's acts of
contrition begin again as if he does not know how to
talk.

The caretaker crosses the courtyard and tells me that
the director wants to see me.

I go to his office. He has me sign several documents. I
notice the Chinese doctor dressed in blue even down
to his striped trousers which seem lighter. The director

picks up the phone and calls out to me:

'The undertakers have just arrived. I will ask them to finally screw down the coffin lid. Do you want to see your Dada one last time before they do?'

I say no. He speaks quietly into the phone and gives an order: I hear him say,

'Tell them they can go ahead.'

Then he informs me he will not be coming to the funeral. He looks around the office as if that is enough explanation. He would send an emissary. He sits down behind his desk and crosses his legs. He explains that the doctor and I would be alone with the nurse on duty. Again his eyes briefly sweep my face like a wind from across the peninsula.

In principle, the residents are not permitted to go to funerals. He only allows them to attend the wake.

'It's easier for them that way,' he says.

But there comes certain strength in the vessels of his throat even as he clears it; he is a man used to giving orders. He has given permission for an elderly friend of Dada's to walk behind the cortege: 'Kim Song,' the director smiles.

'You see:' he tells me, 'it is rather childish, but he and your Dada were hardly ever apart. Here at home, they are teased about it; people would say to Kim: "Is he your special friend?" Then your Dada would laugh and say;'

'Haven't you heard about Saturday nights in the barrel?' 'Then they would both laugh.'

'It made them happy. They had been shipmates together and it's true Dada's death has upset him a great deal. I didn't see how I could refuse him permission. He attended the wake last night.'

I remember it must have been Kim Song staring at me as I awoke. As if he knew my whole story. We sit in silence for some time. The doctor stands up and looks out of the office window. At one point, he remarks: 'Here comes the holy man from the district. He's early.' He explains to me that it would take at least three quarters of an hour to walk to the graveyard. It lies some distance beyond the centre of the village. We go downstairs. The priest and the two assistants who follow him are standing in front of the building. One of them is holding some robes and the little priest bends down to adjust the silver folds. When he arrives, he calls me 'my son' and says a few words to me. He goes inside and I follow him. I notice right away that the screws on the coffin have been tightened and that there are four men in the room also dressed in blue. I'm glad I have the right colours. I still have the patch of red cloth in my pocket and with the blue and the black of my suit and tie, I have the full ticket.

Someone has told me that black and a touch of blue is the right thing to do in Sarawak. You couldn't go wrong that way; the red provides a flourish for the Chinese. I hear the director say that the hearse is waiting out on the road and at the same time the holy man immediately starts to mutter and pray. After that, everything happens very quickly. The men walk over to the coffin and carry a large cloth to cover it. The priest follows behind. The director and I go outside.

The woman stands by the door.

'This is Rana Abdulla,' says the director pointing to me. I didn't catch the woman's name, but immediately know her again, the nurse from Kalimantan, her scarf is black today and she nods a greeting. No smile crosses her long, bony face. Then we all step aside to let the body pass.

'She is here to keep an eye on Kim Song and to make sure he comes to no harm,' the director says.

We follow the pall-bearers out of the home. The hearse waits at the front of the door. The coffin is polished, shiny and oblong and seems too small to carry a man. Beside it stand the chief undertaker and the funeral director, a short man in a ridiculous outfit, and the old man Kim Song who looks a little lost and self-conscious.

I confirm that this is Dada's good friend. He wears a light cap with a round top and a big brim, like you see at baseball games in America. He takes it off as the coffin comes through the door. He has a suit with trousers that hang down over his shoes and a blue bow tie that looks too small for the large collar of his white shirt. This is all I remember. His lips are trembling beneath his nose which is a concertina of wrinkled flesh. He might have been a boxer in his youth.

I remember Dada's stories of Liverpool and being attacked and how they had to duck and weave and wonder if this is his old partner. Against his fine white hair you can see he has odd, misshapen ears that droop down and whose lobes are blood-red and fat which is a sign of good luck and fertile life in China. The light strikes against his lined face. The funeral director tells us where to stand. The priest is at the front, followed by his helpers and the hearse, and around it, the four pall-bearers. Behind them come the doctor and myself and completing the cortege, the nurse and Mr Song.

The sky is already bathed in sunlight. It is beginning to weigh down heavily on the earth and the heat intensifies with every passing minute. I don't know why we wait so long before setting off. I feel hot in my black suit and cap, with a piece of Dada's cloth on my shoulder and I'm glad my mother and father have not attended even though I love my mother. I could not stand their disdain. I wonder what they would think about the old man not only having a formal Chinese funeral but a Catholic one as well. Maybe they would laugh. It would only confirm Dada's betrayal and how they both had to work doubly hard to be Malaysian to mitigate his sins. The thought makes me want to laugh as well; me in my light Malayan skin but with the soul of a pirate and Sea Dayak. Identity is what Borneo is about.

The old man has put his hat back on but now takes it off again to fan himself. I turn slightly towards Kim Song while the doctor tells me about him. He says that my Dada and he often used to walk to the village together in the evening, accompanied by the nurse. Sometimes they took a glass of beer or wine. I look at the country-side all around me. When I see the rows of blue leaved Cypress trees leading into the hills high against the sky, and the green and reddish land, the houses dotted here and there, I understand how peaceful the Dada must have felt here.

Out above the river in the country evenings it must have offered a moment of solace to each day but now the unbroken sun blazing down upon the shimmering landscape makes all of it an oppressed grey, as hot as a molten pan. We start walking. I notice that Kim Song is limping slightly. Gradually, the hearse picks up speed, and the old man starts to lag behind. The hearse passes one of the walkers who has been alongside it. He now walks beside me, as if surprised at how quickly the sun has risen in the sky.

I am conscious that the heat of the country and all its sounds and smells seems to be beating down on me. Since I have only my cap, I fan myself with my piece of red funeral cloth in addition to my handkerchief. The man from the funeral home says something to me that I could not hear. He wipes his head with a handkerchief he holds in his left hand, and pushes up the brim of his hat with the other.

'What did you say?' I ask.

'It's terribly hot,' he repeats and angles his elbow at the sun.

'Yes,' I reply. A moment later, he asks:

'Where is the rain? Is that your grandfather in the coffin?' I say 'Yes.' and wonder why the two questions should come together like that.

'Was he old?' he says. I replied 'Very.' because I don't know exactly how old, but he looks old, especially towards his last days with me. Then the man stops talking as if digging down inside himself for the long walk ahead.

I turn around and think I can see the Dada walking though the shimmering countryside, his image appearing then disappearing like Kim Song's in the ridges of the little hills. A mixture of Sultans Rajahs and Tuns, white men, Sea Dayaks, pirates and slavers walk with him and are overseen by Chinese compradors one of whom carries a whip.

'They told him the story of his birth came about as the son of a Chinese communist who fought and died in the jungle and his acting father was really just some uncle who took pity on his Ma. He didn't find out the truth until much later.' I say.

'He's patriotic to the last,' he replies.

'And yet this own daughter a good Malay girl reflects her ignorance by not being with you here today?' he asks

I wonder how he knows this. I love my mother though with the heat and everything I have become beyond caring. Maybe everyone knows each other's stories out here. I think of the lady in blue and hear her words. 'Your father is fierce in his denunciation of your Dada. He visits me once with your mother. It seems he wants to get on in the machinery of government and Dada is the problem. The suburbs are his dream; he is born in the jungle you know.'

I nod at the floor. Maybe it is all common knowledge. The man stops talking. It makes me grateful. Dada's proud stubbornness has to be beaten down. I wonder if he had attended his own stepfather's funeral.

I want to go back to the city. My home is of the sea pirates, a beautiful yet terrible dream that keeps everything going inside me, their boats full of communists and anarchists although they do not know it then, whose homes are now the suburbs; who are put down by the Rajahs, white and Malay, of course they are, they have to be.

'I'm too mixed,' Dada used to say.

He says all seafarers are the same by skin or colour or creed and none of them know the difference once they sail across the water. My mother keeps quiet at first when he says these things but later in her own way she grew as strident as my father. After she finished university she became worse. She now shares my father's dream. I am an early child and they do not have any more because of the shock. The lady in blue tells me this.

'It would have caused us even more trouble.' my mother says.

'Did you ever love him?' I ask her once.

She says, 'you should ask your Nana that.'

She's going to add something else but stops. Her mother is long dead and there is not much point. Things go cool for me long after my first taste of the rattan cane and then the secret of the Dada's birth.

I hold my cap out in front of me. I try to walk quickly in my own shade but it is impossible. It flaps as I hurry. I look across at the doctor. He walks with a great dignity, every gesture measured and purposeful. He has made this walk before. The clouds gather although the heat is still intense. A few beads of perspiration form on his forehead but he doesn't wipe them away. It seems as if the procession is again moving more quickly. All around me the landscape glares at me like Kim Song at the wake. Suddenly it floods in shadow. Thank God, I say. For a second the brightness becomes unbearable and then come the first welcome drops of rain.

We will be drenched but it breaks the gathered heat that lies in pools around us. At one point, we walk over a section of road that has just been resurfaced. The sun has burned and blistered the tar. Our feet sink down into its shimmering soft mass. What has been exposed to the sun becomes just as quickly susceptible to the rain. The holes begin to fill with puddles. This is our life here; driven mad by the riches given and taken away.

The priest begins to sing. He suddenly produces yellow robes the colour of saffron. Just visible above the hearse, the emissary's hardened leather hat looks as if it has been moulded from the same black material as the bitumen on the road. Raindrops fall from the brim onto his shoulders. I feel a bit lost standing between the early sun and now the leaden sky and the relentless shadowing of these other colours in the yellow light: the sticky black of the water, the sodden road , the dull blue of the mourning clothes, the shine of the hearse, the red flowers that console me with my bearings.

The sun, the rain, the smell of leather and wet grass cling to the wheels of the carriage. A momentary odour of sandalwood and incense assault my nostrils. The exhaustion from not having slept all night stings my eyes and blurs my thoughts. I turn again: the doctor looks very far away, fading into a cloudy haze of steaming heat until he appears as blurred as a mirage before my eyes. When the rain comes it washes away any trace or image of the Dada. He no longer appears through the folds of the earth.

I notice that the road in front of me is on a curve. Kim Song knows the area and has taken a short cut to catch up with us. By the time we come around the bend he is behind us again. Then we lose sight of him. He takes another country path and does the same thing several times over, rising up and down like the pitching of a ship. I can feel the blood pumping in my temples and everything that is happening goes at a snail's pace and yet passes so quickly, even the daylight from blistering sun to heavy rain seems to weigh against my steaming clothes like a stone. A feeling of solace comes and goes with it. A freshness comes into the air at departure of the rain but a part of me shivers even in the heat It is difficult to remember anything about the ceremony itself except one comment stands out. As we are entering the village, the nurse speaks to me. She has an unusual voice that seems inconsistent with her strong face, a trembling, persecuted, Kalimantan voice.

'If you walk too slowly;' she says, 'you risk getting sun stroke. But if you go too quickly even with this rain, you're sweating by the time you reach the church and then you catch a chill.'

She's right. It makes sense but all I can think of is the pimp who beats her. There is no escaping the fact that it could be Iskra or one of his friends.

Certain other moments stay with me. The look of triumph on Kim Songs face as he catches up with us for the last time near the village, great tears of fear and pain flow down his cheeks. Because he has so many wrinkles, they collect there. They form little pools in the furrows of his devastated forehead, covering it in a glistening film of water like the tar pools on the road. I feel sorry for him but I also feel glad. It is wonderful to have someone love you so much. The way you are always protected when you have been through something with someone, a resistance, an uprising, a trip outside of the ordinary matters of the day where everything is unimportant seems suddenly to dissolve. I can see why he and the Dada are such friends.

Then the grave, the plot freshly dug on the hillside where the Dada can look out over the sea. I do not say to home because his face might as well be turned to Europe the way he spoke of the Blue Funnel Line and its great diaspora among the Chinese seamen. Borneo bore him but you would not think so the way my father used to speak of his betrayal.

'One who does not deserve to belong among us,' he

says.

Village people come out onto the streets. Red geraniums are sprinkled all the way up to the graveside to clear the ground of ghosts. In the little cemetery area, there is a moment when someone faints. They sink like a puppet doll collapses to the stage when the master releases the strings.

The earth – the colour of blood even through the puddles – the throwing of wood, red cloths and smoke over Dada's coffin, the soft white of the blue and black and yellow robes, the smell of cologne and tobacco all mix together, a great perfume that the Catholics offer the Dada who in turn becomes their link to the sea. More people, more voices, the village is comforting me as it would with any of its fallen. It would not let me stand alone. I am struck by being very grateful. This is a place I can visit.

In front of the cafe, comes the relentless drone of voices, the clatter of coffee saucers and the occasional clink of glass. Suddenly I hear the roar of the bus engine in the square. My joy when at last it would pull me away from here and some hours later deposit me into the clouds of dust and red lights that is the city of Kuching and I would see again where the river winds like a golden thread through the different kampongs and all its districts, makes me sad and glad at the same time.

I know now I can go home soon and lie down and sleep for twelve hours and all the following day if I want. I also know I need something to calm me, to smoke some weed or jangle a piece of rock to soothe me into the calm of the night. It is like the music in the clubs; forget the sudden furious dancing; only afterwards would come the darkness and tranquillity of the sea and the easy dawn. These events have drained me. How am I to know within this exhaustion that I would meet Mo or that I would help my neighbour Iskra with his lover or if Old Srino would not bother me relentlessly about his bird? How little I know that Iskra's knife will be used to hang me, hang me, screaming and resistant under a grey and brooding Malaysian morning; or that others would come to me with their stories of death and luck and history that would be turned against me as much as the tide of Dada's traitorous acts. Everything is pure chance. None of this means anything to me as I put my head to the pillow and dream few thoughts but instead fall into a deep sonorous sleep beneath the window where you can hear the tack, tack, tack, of the rain.

Chapter Eleven

Slow Sunday

I can't remember much of the following day. I sleep most of it, stepping into and out of incessant dreams and rain. On Sunday after waking early, I think of all the people who used to come to the apartment when Dada lives here. I cannot remember any of them well. On mornings like these the eggs would come straight out of the frying pan if he has no bread then he would wander around the large apartment. He loves the space. He used to say he liked the sound of his feet padding on the floor.

'Sunday is the same as any other day at sea.' he says. He has never been used to space with his life spent in the engine rooms and stokeholds of his many ships. Space is important he says, it allows him to pace and wander and to call down to all his friends, a real freedom for anyone used to confined spaces.

'To make your bed is to clear space in your head,' he would say.

He moves the dining table into the side room and

makes me live in my bedroom and stay in this one room with its few straight chairs. He takes the comfortable mattress as his own and leaves me his closet with its yellowing mirror, a dressing table and the blue and white coverlet over the sheet, a remnant from the fleets of Alfred Jones and the Borneo Steamship Company. He says when I come to live here everything has to have its place. Nothing should be left after you had used it, but folded and put away, less you would always be chasing after your immediate past and that is not important.

'You need space if you want to draw big pictures, that are the stuff that defines you,' he would say.

He constantly uses the empty room to pace about and to call out to the street. He has his scrap books that he would get out or cut and paste something from the papers that amuses him just like it does my boss.

He has hundreds of these old notebooks. He studies them sometimes when he's eating and crumbs would fall down onto their ridged and crumpled paper. I see a photograph of a young woman in one of them. When he has finished his meal he would wash his hands and go out on to the balcony where he would shout out his thoughts to the street. Short of the visits from the detectives, those who lived around here learned to pay him little attention.

The balcony looks out over the main street of the neighbourhood. He would stay there for hours on beautiful Sunday afternoons. People who passed by might be in a hurry but he would call down to them just the same.

'Do you know what they're up to now,' he would roar.

There are many families who go out for a walk for their Sunday afternoon. Little boys wear their best suits and shorts with shiny shoes or the girls in little sarongs that drape delicately down to their ankles. They look a little awkward in their formal clothes – got up like this with one little girl with a large pink bow in her hair and black patent-leather shoes who flashes her eyes from side to side as if expecting everyone to laugh.

Behind them comes their mother, an enormous woman in a brown silk sarong, and their father, a rather frail-looking, short man I'd seen before. He wears a suit and tie even in this heat and carries an umbrella for the rain to come. Seeing them together, I understand why Dada says they look distinguished, the way the woman carries herself.

'She brings them dignity.' he says.

I need some air. I slowly walk out of the apartment and along the quays. I catch up with the same family a little while later alongside the parading local young men who pass me by: slicked-back hair, red ties, very tight jackets with embroidered handkerchiefs sticking out of their pockets and shoes with square toes. They are probably going to see a movie in town after their *promenade* that is why they are leaving so early and laughing so much as they hurry to catch the bus. After they'd gone, the quays gradually become deserted.

The sky grows darker as I walk home and I think of the summer storms to come without him. It draws a cloud over my mood. His laugh does not make me feel better, just more alone. Dada says that in Australia it stays sunny for weeks and even months. Here the sun is always broken by the rain and mist even in high summer. You can never take a chance or go for days without protection. This time by some miracle the sky has cleared again and for an instant a beautiful green light settles over the harbour. The constantly passing clouds have left the threat of a downpour hovering above the street but just at this moment it has a rare beauty. I stand still and look up at the sky for a long time and watch the rain slowly form in sheaths from the black underbellies of the clouds as they ride like ships going away to the sea.

The vans and buses of the sports team come back at nearly six o'clock and make a lot of noise. The smart guys and young men have been to the stadium in the suburbs and the buses carry groups of spectators who are huddled on the running boards and hanging on to the guardrails. The next one is full of the players. I recognize them by their bags. They are shouting and singing at the top of their lungs - their club would go on forever and songs of individuals and beautiful players. Several of them wave to me; one even calls out:

'We thrashed them Rana your Dada would be proud!'

I nod my head and say 'Yes.'

After that, more and more traffic began streaming by in an endless exit from the city after this quiet time. The clouds still gather.

Dada is a strange man, everyone knows him but he is still strange. He laughs a lot. He seems stranger when the Malays cannot place him and the Chinese turn their head to one side in that way they have but the Indonesians love him. They call him Sam even though his name is Kim the same as his shipmate Mr Song. He laughs with everyone. He tells me he has to, what is the alternative? When the Chinese down below threaten to throw him overboard or burn him with their shovels, when his wife says he is more Chinese than Malay, when his own daughter leaves him or when the bitter word Dayak enters the room, what else could he do?

He says he has bad dowager stock served upon him from the day he's born. What else can you do but laugh. He even marries a Malay girl to be accepted. But that has gone wrong, he chuckles again. Those who laugh at tragedy only stoke up their own dementia, someone tells me later but only after I learn not to be afraid. There is no mention of another child.

'Too many years have washed my soul.' he used to say.

The shroud of shame follows him to this final village even if it does not deter him. He carries on, makes new friends, drinks his brandy, tells his stories, walks out in the evening, and sings his songs. Everyone knows him from his time on the balcony or when people come up to the apartment but he has to be careful. He laughs with everyone but only the Kalimantans and other immigrants really understand his jokes. Nothing to him appears sacred, everything profane and even when that changes and he becomes tired, his lips still could not resist a chuckle.

He laughs at the officials and governors of this blighted island and even more at the white Rajahs before them with their family kingdoms served in perpetuity by the Borneo Steam Packet Company; orders adhered to and continued by the Sultans and Tuns, little wonder he laughs. He could talk of Australasia more than any boss of mine and says he believed in it especially the Catholic outback west. He is full of stories and a stranger to his own family. His jokes go with him to the grave.

I remember them all. Time passes. I return home.

Above the rooftops, the sky has grown from green to grey and then to a streaked red. As night falls the streets start filling up again. The people who'd gone out came back, a few at a time, some in better repair than others. I recognize the distinguished-looking family. The children are either crying or letting them- selves be dragged along. The man holds one of them by the hair; the one who has sailed out in her best clothes and looks like a little movie star is all bedraggled. Her screams bounce off the walls. Behind him, his wife sails up the pavement like a galleon on a calm sea.

I look into the face of a young girl whose photograph lies within the folds of Dada's belongings they have packed at the Home. His scrawled writing on the back dates it to the time of his imprisonment. I think of the little Indonesian woman and her son sitting on the floor and whispering to each other, the woman in the scrapbook older, but with the same eyes.

'Goodbye mama.'

'A baby passed over,' the woman in blue has the same piercing eyes.

The cinemas suddenly let out a wave of spectators into the street, all at the same time. Some of the young men are more animated than usual, which makes me think they'd seen a detective thriller. The people coming back from the movies in town arrive a bit later. They look more serious. They are laughing, but only every now and again. They seem tired and preoccupied. They linger in the street and everyone knows that Monday is waiting for us all. They are coming and going on the pavement opposite. The young girls from the neighbourhood walk together wearing their hijabs loose and with their lips rouged. The young men position themselves so the girls would have to pass directly by. They make friendly and encouraging remarks and the girls giggle.

Work like the rain would arrive soon enough. Only pirates think different, little wonder the rulers categorise them as 'vagabonds, no-goods, shy, indolent and bold who have to be made to change for the benefit of the nation.'

The street lights suddenly come on, softening the stars in the night sky. I feel my eyes starting to hurt after watching for so long the changing light and masses of people who swirl by. The lights make the damp pavements glisten and the trees seem greener. Every few minutes the headlights of a bus would light up someone's clothes or hair fallen down from under a scarf, a smile or a silver bracelet that suddenly passes into shadow like a film.

The trams pass by less and less but I still remain by the long window. The house is empty with only me here but it would not be the case for long. Someone would always rent Dada's room. You can't get these old apartments any more and the landlord would be glad of the money. Any diversion keeps me from thinking of his footsteps; even those of my father serve a purpose in distracting me.

The night grows darker above the trees and lights and the streets below began to empty little by little, until I see the first cat slowly cross the street and scratch itself, then the road becomes deserted once more.

I think I should have some supper. My legs ache a little from stopping so much on the way home and then pacing the floor. I buy some bread and noodles and prepare my meal with a hot pepper sauce. I eat it in a bowl while still standing at the window. I unwrap some chocolate and smoke another cigarette. It is cooler now and I feel a little uncomfortable. I close the windows against the river and the stars the way Dada used to do.

As I step back into the room, I see reflected in the mirror, at the edge of the table some bits of bread lying next to Dada's old storm lamp. They must have lain there since I had set off for his funeral. On their own they look like the offerings of a communion taken that day. He has kept the lamp as he had the clock for so many years and would tell stories around it in the winter monsoon how he had swung it so many times in dark alleyways to light his passage.

Now here is Sunday nearly over and I still have not examined the drugs we bought off the boats at Setubong. It is a good sign. I do not want to smoke alone even though it is easy now with the Dada not here. I search for some silver foil but without heart. There is none anyway. I give up. He is dead and buried now and I am back at work tomorrow. When all said and done, nothing more can pass between us except his spirit. Our life goes on and nothing really changes.

A sound comes from outside the door and I turn the lock and look out. Old Srino stands there and stares at his feet. His scabby hands are shaking. Without looking at me, he asks: 'Tell me Rana Abdullah they won't take him away from me will they? They'll give him back to me won't they? Otherwise, what will happen to me?' I tell him that the police keep all live animals for three days in case their owners come for them and that afterwards they do what they think is best. He looks at me in silence. Then he says: 'Good night.' He closes his door and I could hear him walking back and forth. His bed creaks. Then I hear a strange little sound coming from the other side of the wall and I realize he is crying. Dada fills my thoughts. I know I have to get up early to arrange the final documents of his passing. I think of the photograph amongst his papers and the mountain of scrapbooks belonging to his past.

Chapter Twelve

I meet Mo

When I arrive on the quay everywhere bustles in the sunshine. I have overslept. I understand now why my boss doesn't seem happy when I ask for time off. I had more or less forgotten that but realize it all of a sudden when he brings it up again. He must have thought I'd have four days off, including the weekend which he wouldn't have liked at all. But then, it's not every day you go to a funeral. It doesn't mean I can't understand why he's not happy. If we are not working hard he always gets upset. He has said a couple of times now that I have no direction in life.

I had difficulty getting up because the funeral has worn me out. I can still see the Dada's coffin in the sun and then the rain then the sun again, then listening to Old Srino and his worries about his bird. I wonder if I shouldn't go for a swim at lunchtime to clear my head. As soon as the busy period finishes and the merchants have gone and there are just the women waiting in their summer wraps for the cheap fish, I take the trolleybus to the municipal swimming pool near the port. I dive straight into one of the lanes. There are a lot of young people around. In the water, I see Mo al Saleh who used to work at the port office. I found him attractive at the time. I think it's mutual but he did not stay for long so we didn't have time to do anything about it. He sees me and waves.

I help him climb onto a floating platform and my hand brushes against his stomach; my feet still dangle in the water. He's already turned over with his back to the light and stretches out on the platform. He turns towards me. His long hair has fallen over his eyes and he starts to laugh.

I hoist myself up next to him. I'm feeling better after all last week's disturbance. Pretending it to be a bit of a joke, I drop my head back and let it rest next to his belly. He doesn't say anything but he doesn't freeze so I don't move either. You have to be careful being so close to the city. I could see all of the sky above me, blue and golden as a flower. I can feel Mo's ribs beneath me, moving gently as he breathes in and out. We stay that way for a long time, half asleep. When the sun becomes too hot, he jumps into the water and I follow him. I catch up with him, put my arm around his waist and we swim like that together. He brushes me away into the next lane, still laughing. On the poolside, while we are drying off, he says:

'I'm more used to danger than you, so watch yourself.' I ask him if he wants to go to the movies tonight. He laughs again and says he wants to see a film with Tom Hanks in it. I have to hurry back to work but I feel good. By the evening, Mo seems to have forgotten about being careful. He's surprised to see me carrying a red piece of material in my pocket and asks if I am in mourning. I tell him that my Dada has died.

'When did that happen?' he asks.

'Friday,' I say, but I meant I buried him then.

He shudders. For a moment he doesn't say anything. I want to ask him what else could I do and say that death is a part of life but I stop myself because I remember I'd already said that to my boss. And Iskra has said it to me. It doesn't do any good to keep repeating yourself. It's just one of those phrases that don't mean much. Anyone you lose is also a little bit guilty for someone else's death. It's as much about what you don't do as what you do. Some are guiltier than others. Look at my father; he kills the Dada with his absences and influence over my Mother's affections.

The movie is funny in parts but then gets really stupid and melodramatic. Mo is weeping. He presses himself against me. I stroke his cheek. Towards the end of the movie, I kiss him, but awkwardly so no one can see me. After we leave, he comes back with me to Dada's. When I wake up, he's gone. He tells me he has to visit his brother who has some good weed. I realize that it's Tuesday, which annoys me because I still have to work to make up the lost time. Tuesday is such a slow day, a day neither here nor there. I have never liked it. I turn over briefly in bed to see if I can still smell the salt from Mo's hair on the pillow but because we are expecting a heavy trawl, I could not go back to sleep; even though I'm still tired. I work and don't even have time for a proper lunch at the café which is just as well. They would ask too many questions and who I'd seen at the funeral.

Dada's the same. He doesn't like it when people ask

him questions.

'I have my own opinions the same as anyone else,' he used to say.

He'd be cool with anyone who asked him personal stuff but he'd talk about politics and the union all day long. He could be tolerant given all the time he had spent with the detectives, in prison or doing his 'corrective time' that lasted many years longer. Sometimes talk came around of another daughter but I had never met her and nor did my mother say anything...

The white Rajah asks his parents to bring him to the house, the governor's chateau that has ruled this part of the island for over a hundred years. His stepfather attends with his wife and son. The house has a pale blue wooden fence waist high around the perimeter and is constructed in the style of a country house of southern France though the Dada does not know this at the time.

There are rose bushes in the garden and gushing pools of water with red and black carp swimming in them. The house looks down over the harbour where the Rajah's ancestors have arrived from their adventurer's ship. When his stepfather has given his report of the production on the estate up country, the Rajah puts his hand up to signal a pause.

'How is your family?' he asks.

Dada tells me he can feel his stepfather's eyes flicker over himself and his mother. Their faces are turned down as they have been instructed.

'Let me see your eyes boy,' my Dada raises his chin. The Rajah looks at him calmly.

'Very good,' he says. 'Very good, you can tell everything by the eyes.'

He raises his hand again to signal the time for the meeting to end. The smell of roses and sweet grass comes in through the window. They have been in the room for less than five minutes.

'Don't expect me to confide to others my humiliation.' he says.

But towards the end he tells me more stories as if he can't get them off his chest quick enough. One comes from his own mother before the time of the white rajahs and her poor suffering. When the whole of the south of the island becomes threatened by a plague of sword-fish, the fishermen are faced with ruin. A young, poor bright boy the son of a sea Dayak comes forward to the Sultan with a solution. Knowing the way the con-flux of the river meets with the sea, the boy suggests changing the way the nets are laid against the flow of the tide at that particular time of the monsoon. When this works, success is confirmed and the crisis comes to an end, the Sultan sends presents to the boy and his father. He then calls his prime minister to him and tells him to send two trusted guards and to go and kill the boy and his old man. The prime minister chafes against this order.

'But the boy did us all a great favour.' he says.

'No.' the Sultan says.

'No.' he repeats, 'The boy thought and spoke above his station and causes a rift in the natural order of things. I rule by divine right and you preside over day to day matters because I have delegated you that right. If we let excellence decide promotion and start to judge peo-ple by worth and not by birth, this society will collapse throughout Malaya and for all Malays I cannot allow that.'

'That is the way they think,' Dada says. 'Even today it is what they believe deep down.' He gives me a fierce look.

I can picture him now in full flow; see him with the sunlight on the water from our place on the wharf; from our balcony when he stumbles and has taken a drink but nothing can stop his voice.

'Lee Kwan Yew in Singapore has experience of this situation,' he'd shout. 'He knows the happenings of what goes on in Borneo. He can see us seamen only wish to address the situation. He understands the Sultans and Rajahs and Tuns would all want their place back after the imperialists have gone home. And our place is *down*. We are the outsiders here because we exist inside and outside of their frontiers. Are we meant to think less of our own nation when we absent ourselves for bread and identity? Our passports and identity cards reveal nothing about us.'

'You must listen to history,' the Dada says.

He rolls his blue cigarette papers in the breeze and looks me directly in the eye, then he pauses and shudders as if a ghost has walked across his grave.

'My family too they scorn me. I am Dayak and Chinese, I marry Malay and we have your mother. We are here before any of them come to divide this place. She is Malay. She is fiercely Malay. They think that I betray the Federation by bringing out the seamen. We care for all the seamen, not just the Chinese but the Dayaks and Malay, even the Kalimantan. We are all one in the pockets of the Borneo Steamship Company.' His eyes are somewhere else.

'They say I squander my birthright. They forbid me from family. They jail and beat me but what do I have in

common with Peking or Kuala Lumpur, Rome or Mecca? I am a Borneo seaman. A man of the Sunda Islands, a common working man they call a Communist.'
'And what of this woman, your other daughter?' I ask.
'She is with me all through those terrible times but now she too has gone.' His voice becomes quiet.
I cook myself some eggs and eat them at the back of the shop which pleases my boss. He can see I am trying to catch up after the funeral. After lunch I pull a chair outside the shop and only get up when someone wants to buy. Most families would be home now. Even the boss keeps glancing at his watch. His wife would not tolerate any late arrival. He'd leave me in charge. At this time of the day, I could read from the newspapers that he buys that so enrage and amuse him. He has marked the exchanges between the Government and the Thai politicians and the immigrant fishermen who use the Burmese women on their illegal ships to fill our harbours with drugs and prostitution. It does his business no harm.
'Life gets messy in any walk of life,' he says. 'You cook your own goose but you can benefit from anything if you find a way around it.'
I see the woman in blue with her little sparrow face and the way she rubs her earrings between her thumb and forefinger as if summoning up some genie. No wonder Dada always goes quiet when you ask him personal stuff.
'We are all strangers to each other.' he says.

Chapter Thirteen

Iskra's letter

Work is was always hard at the warehouse. We keep the fish frozen at our unit on the wharf but the merchant house, as they call it, stores all the grain and herbs and plants we sell further up the quay. They send all the produce around the local river kampongs and the entire district but it still remains only city based. This is why the boss wants to expand, given the dynamics of the industry.

'People just don't want something lying on the slab any more,' he says, 'it reminds them of their own death. You need to garnish everything these days.'

There has been good catches off them fucking Thai boats. My boss appears pleasant towards me. He asks if Dada's death hasn't washed me out and his age when he passed away. I say in his eighties so I wouldn't make a mistake. I don't know why, but he seems relieved and considers the matter closed.

'How many kids did he have?' he asks suddenly.

I stumble on that one but it doesn't seem to matter as

he only laughs.

'Seamen are always the same,' he says.

Bills of lading are piled up in a stack on a desk in the back and I go through them all. At twelve noon I wash my hands before leaving the shop for lunch. I like this moment of the day. In the evening, it's not as nice because the shop is like a wasteland and all the towels are soaking wet. They have been used all day long and the fish has left its smell above the ice. I point this out to the boss. He says sorry but in the end it is only a minor detail and is not important for the running of the business.

'Besides,' he says, 'all you smell in the morning is fresh disinfectant. The merchant house is always perfumed in its dealings with the public.'

With talking, I go out a little late, at twelve thirty, with Abdul Hassan who works in the shipping office down the quay. The office looks out over the river and we spend a moment watching the cargo ships coming into the port, their decks bathed in the scorching sun.

Just then, a truck arrives with racket of rattling chains and what sounds like explosions from its engine boxes. It carries a stack of wire and wooden lobster crates they use for the luxury trade. Abdul asks if we should go for it and I start to run. The truck rushes past and we chase after it. The noise and dust is blinding. I can barely see a thing but I put my foot down. All I feel is the exhilarating rush as we sped between the winches and machinery, past the masts of the fishing boats and small coasters bobbing up and down on the wharf. In the distance, cargo and container ships with their hulls daubed with signs of Kojo Lines or Ned Lloyd and Maersk lie at anchor towards Setubong. They are like magic signs from across the sea the way Dada used to talk.

I take a huge leap and manage to jump on the truck. Then I help Hassan climb up. We are gasping for breath as we bump along the uneven cobblestones of the quayside in the sun and dust. Hassan is laughing so hard he can hardly breathe. By the time we get to Jamila's, we are bathed with sweat. She is always there, with her fat stomach, her apron and her laughing smile. She asks me if everything is OK. Yes I say but I'm hungry and she laughs some more. I eat very quickly and then I take a coffee. Afterwards I go home and sleep a little because I am heavy with the lunch and tired from the running. When I wake up, I immediately feel like having a cigarette.

I work all through the afternoon, It is very hot in the shop and in the evening, when I leave, I take a walk slowly back home, through the rain and steaming pavements. The sunset would be great tonight and I want to watch it from my window and also because I want to make myself some boiled cabbage and put a little distance between my weekend and the promise of drugs. My mouth is as bitter as fallen stars.

As I walk up the stairs, I run into Old Srino, a neighbour who lives on the same floor as me. He holds his parrot's cage. The bird is always with him. He's had him for years and they always go out together. The bird has a skin disease – mange, I think it's called – which makes him lose almost all his feathers. It leaves him covered in reddish patches and brown scabs. Because they've lived together for so long in one little room, Old Srino has ended up looking like his bird. He also has reddish scabs on his face and in his yellowish, thinning hair.

When the bird needs to shit, the old man doesn't give him enough time to finish and he pulls at the cage so the bird leaves a trail of little drops on the wire. If the bird accidentlally pees in the room beyond his perch the old man flies at him with a rolled up newspaper, his perch is rattled again. They say it's been going on like this for years.

Like any animal the bird has taken on some of his owner's characteristics. He hunches up with his neck sticking out and his muscles tense. They look like they're related and yet they hate each other. Twice a day, at noon and six o'clock, the old man carries the cage out with the bird inside down to the pavement for a change of air; Dada says for eight years, they haven't changed their routine. You can see Srino walking down to the café, the bird calls out; the old man slams the cage and curses him. He lugs the cage home, sweating and cursing. This happens two or three times on their excursions. As soon as the bird has forgotten and sees the open cage he hops out and performs his ablutions. This pulls his master's rag again and he curses and rattles the bars even though he should be grateful. Then the two of them stand still on the pavement and look at each other, the bird with terror, and the old man with hatred. It is the same every day. And now the bird is lost the old man is the one who is terrified.

Jalima says: 'It's awful but why does he open the cage, if I did that with the tax man, everyone would be after me.'

'To show him what freedom looks like.' I say.

'But when all is said and done, no one really knows what freedom is.' she says.

When I run into them on the stairs, Srino is always cursing the bird. He calls him 'bastard!' and 'dirty swine!' and the bird chatters with fear. I say: 'Good evening,' but the old man keeps on shouting at his pet. I ask him what's the parrot done but he doesn't reply. All he says is, 'Bastard' and 'dirty swine!' over and over. He is bent at the cage, trying to untangle a pink ribbon that has become entwined with the wire bars, the same ribbon that is shot with grey at the bird's unexplained explosions. I speak louder and ask him what the bird has done.

Without looking up Srino replies with a sort of repressed rage:

'He's always fucking here.'

Then he leaves, holding the cage up with the terrified bird inside, whimpering and talking in a low voice, as maddened as his owner.

Just as I close the door and lie down on the bed and wait for that cool time when the sun leaves the window after the rain, Iskra knocks for me. He has lived a long time in this building. Rumour has it that he lives off women. But when you ask him what he does, he says he works in a warehouse at the docks just like me. He's not very well liked around here but you could say the same about Dada. He often talks to me and from time to time he drops by for a while because I listen to him just like I do with old Srino. I find what he says interesting. And besides, I don't have any reason not to talk to him. He's short with broad shoulders, thick, hairy arms and a boxer's nose. He's always very well dressed.

Once, when we are talking about Srino he says, 'that's a terrible thing that goes on there.

'Don't you find it all very disgusting?' he says.

'No,' I say, 'everyone has to have something to hold onto.'

I do not tell him about my pirate's life or of my history. He might think my rebellion is based only against the power of my parents. I don't want him to think that. He might imagine all I don't want to talk is boiled down to this, just like my cabbage.

As Iskra goes to leave and walk back to his apartment he says: 'I've got some lamb's kidneys inside and wine. Would you like to have a bite to eat with me?'

I thought how I wouldn't have to cook dinner; forget about my cabbage and the sunset. I say yes.

Iskra only has one room and a kitchen with a small window. On the wall above his bed there's a pink and white stucco angel and some pictures of sporting champions, the fighter Manny Pacquino from the Philippines and two or three snapshots of semi naked women. The room is not very clean and he hasn't made the bed. First he switches on the supplementary lights and the room flickers yellow, then he takes a used elasticated support bandage out of his pocket and pulls it up and over his right hand. He holds it into a fist and flexes it until just his stubby fingers are showing beyond the fabric.

I ask him what has happened. He tells me he's been in a fight with some guy who has been asking for trouble. 'You have to understand, Rana,' he says.

'I'm not a bad sort but I do have a quick temper. So this guy says to me: ""If you're really a man, you'll get off this bus", so I say: "Come on now, don't get so worked up." Then he calls me a coward. So I get off and I tell him: "That's enough now. Cut it out or you'll have this."'

He holds up the fist with the elastic bandage around it, cracked and dirty in the low light...

'The guy says: "you and who else?" So I punch him. He falls down.

'I want to help him up but he starts kicking me while still on the ground. So I hit him with my knee and punch him a few times. His face is all bloody. I ask him if he's had enough. He says "Yes."'

'Take this handkerchief,' I say to him, 'clean yourself up.'

All the time he's talking, Iskra is rubbing the bandage on his hand. I am sitting on the bed.

'You can see that I don't go looking for trouble,' he says, 'he's the one who starts it.'

This rings true and I say so. Then he tells me that he actually wants my advice on the whole business, that I seem like a man who understands life, how I could help him and afterwards he'd be my friend. I don't reply. He asks me again if I'd like to be his friend. I tell him that I don't mind. He seems pleased. He takes out the kidneys from a newspaper wrapping and starts cooking them in a frying pan. He puts out the glasses, plates, cutlery and two bottles of wine all in silence. Then we sit down at the table. While we are eating, he starts telling me his story.

At first he hesitates, 'I used to know this woman... I guess you could call her my mistress,' the man he has had the fight with is the woman's brother. He tells me that he's been keeping her. I don't say anything and right away he adds that he knows what people say about him in the neighbourhood but he works in a warehouse and has a clear conscience.

'But to get on,' he says, 'I realize she's cheating on me.'

He gives her enough money to live on. He even pays her rent and gives her another fifty a day for food.

'Three hundred Ringo for her room, six hundred for going out and a pair of stockings now and again and all that adds to more than a thousand.'

'That's a few dollars,' he says, 'and, needless to say, Madame doesn't work but she tells me she can't get by on what I give her.

'So I ask her: "Why not get a job, just part time. That would help me out because all those other little things add up. I bought you a new outfit this month, I give you nearly twenty dollars a day, I pay your rent and what do you do? You go to the café in the afternoon with all your friends from Kalimantan. You offer them coffee and almond sugar cakes while I'm the one giving you money. I've been good to you but you haven't been good to me."

'But she doesn't go out to work, she keeps saying she couldn't and that's when I realize she must be cheating on me.'

Iskra then tells me how he'd found a series of lottery tickets in her bag and how she couldn't explain where she'd got the money to buy them. A little later he finds a pawn ticket and a receipt for two gold bracelets. Up until then, he doesn't even know if she's owned any jewellery, not like that stuff anyway.

'That's when I know for sure she's been cheating on me. So I go to leave. But first, I hit her. Then I tell her the truth about herself. I tell her that all she really wants is to get laid and it doesn't matter by whom.

'You understand, Rana Abdullah,' he says, 'I say to her, you don't see how jealous everyone is of you and how happy I've made you. You'll realize later on how happy you were with me.'

He's beaten her before then but he's never really hit her.

'I slapped her a little, but affectionately, so to speak. She'd cry a bit but then I'd close the shutters and it would finish the way it always does. But now it's serious. And as far as I'm concerned, I haven't punished her enough.' He then explains that is why he needs my advice.

He stops talking to fix the lighting which flickers in shadows on the wall. Just beyond the window, I can see the far streaks of sunset as the sky turns black. It makes me happy and I just sit and listen to him. I have taken a glass of wine and my forehead feels very hot.

Iskra turns away from the stove. 'I liked your Dada,' he says, 'but there was something wrong about him.' I hear something move inside me.

'Fuck off.' I say.

'Something, I can't get my head around what.' he says. 'Where is the other girl?' he asks.

'I don't know.' I say.

I smoke some more of his cigarettes because I don't have any of my own left. The last buses pass by, carrying away the distant sounds of the suburbs. Iskra continues talking. What bothers him is he still has sexual feelings for the woman. But he still wants to punish her. First he'd thought he'd take her to a hotel and call the Vice Squad to cause a scandal and have her officially registered as a prostitute. Then he'd gone to see some shady friends of his but they couldn't come up with anything. And as he points out, petty criminals are never much good and if you do use them, you are always in their debt. He's forgotten the Dada.

He tells them the same story and when they'd suggest 'branding' her or breaking her legs, he knows they know nothing. Anyway he doesn't like the idea of violence or being in their keep. He needs to think about it. First, however, he wants to ask me something. Before he does though, he wants to know what I think about the whole business. I tell him I don't really have any opinion about it, but that I find it interesting.

Then he asks me if I think she has been cheating on him and I say that yes, it seems that way to me. He wants to know if I think she should be punished and what would I do if I were him. I tell him that you can never know for sure because chance plays such a big part in these things, but I can understand why he wants to punish her. People are always punishing others, look at my Dada but I don't say anything to Iskra about that. I drink some more wine. Iskra lights a cigarette and tells me his plan. He wants to write her a letter, one that would 'hit her hard but at the same time say things that would make her sorry and miss him.' Then, after she came back to him, he'd sleep with her and as soon as he'd finished, he'd spit in her face and throw her out. I tell him I think that would be a good way to punish her without any violence.

'It makes you wonder if we don't all cheat on each other,' Iskra says.

But he doesn't think he'll be able to write the kind of letter that is needed, that's why he wants me to do it. When I don't reply, he asks if I wouldn't mind doing it right then and there. Strangely I agree. He drinks another glass of wine and stands up a little unsteady. He pushes aside our plates and the last of the kidneys and carefully cleans the tablecloth of any crumbs. He gets a sheet of lined paper out of the drawer of his bedside table, along with a yellow envelope and a fountain pen, - a little penholder made of red wood and a square inkwell filled with purple ink makes up the set.

'You don't want a computer when you have something serious to write.' he says.

Iskra tells me the women's name. I realize straight away she's from one of the districts of Kalimantan, probably the north. It's poorest there and they are always burning wood to keep themselves warm. It makes the land even cheaper. You can smell it across all of Sarawak when the wind blows towards the West, even though we are the Eastern States, it shows you how fucked up it all is here. I write the letter. I more or less improvise, but I try to write it in a way that would make Iskra happy and make the girl think it has come from him. I have no reason not to make him happy.

I remember Dada's words, 'In between their Federations and Republics, we are no more than puppets, carved out as simply as the British, the Dutch and Japanese have carved us; no more the East Indies than the Spice Islands. There's nothing between us and their borders. Whenever we think we know who we are, there is always someone here to tell us different.'

I read the letter out to him. Iskra smokes as he listens; nodding his head, and then asks me to read it again. He seems really pleased.

'I can tell you understood life,' he says warmly.

I don't realise at first but he starts addressing me in a very personal way. It only strikes me when he says: 'Now, we're really pals.' He says the same again and I say: 'Yes we are.'

It doesn't mean much to me one way or the other but it

really seems to matter to him. He puts the letter in an envelope and we finish the wine. Then we sit there for a while, smoking in silence. Outside, everything has become quiet and you could only hear the isolated sound of a car passing by.

I say, 'It's late.' He thinks so too.

He remarks that time passes quickly here in the tropics, a man's life could disappear between monsoons he says and, in a certain way it's true, what happens between May and November can lead you to think there is another life awaiting you. I'm tired though and find it difficult to get out of my chair. I must have looked done in because Iskra says I should take better care of myself. At first I don't understand. Then he says he's sorry to hear that Dada has passed away.

'Was he Chinese?' he asks. Then he covers himself and says, 'It's just something that people say, they don't really know.'

'No,' I say, 'he just acted that way.'

I stand up; Iskra shakes my hand very hard and says that we men must always understand each other. He asks me if I want to stay there the night with him but I say no.

'Good night.' I say to him.

He slaps my shoulder, 'Goodnight my little gangster.' he says.

'I can see you were a good student.'

I close his door behind me when I leave and stand on the landing for a moment in the dark. I think of Dada and the letter and what had come to pass to bring him into the world. I don't like to talk about this nor my hallucinations, or the stain, they say resides within our family but his voice sounds strong within me and chimes all the way down the hall.

'It has nothing to do with who you are,' he used to say. 'prison is just one of these places life brings you to.'

I can hear his laughter bounce from wall to wall and his stories, more of them as he becomes weaker as if he's telling me tales against himself and what might have been different or what he could have done different.

'We come out of the Malay club in Liverpool. We're going to town for a drink. We're making jokes, laughing. We are going to see our mates in Great Nelson Street. The Chinese bars are there and they play Mahjong in the upstairs rooms of the restaurants but they don't mind who goes there. They are not in the engine room now. You can hear them banging down the numbers, drinking and swearing on any sunny afternoon in that city. They love the white girls, especially the Irish. They treat them like queens. The pub is like the shipping office for the Blue Funnel. Two white guys come up to us. "Hey Chinky, Chinky." they say. We're smiling, bowing, backing off.

'They act with purpose. One hits my friend full on his face. I think of Kim Song and his broken nose.

'I detain the other. We go into our routine ducking the punches, to dance and feint like we had been taught. I hope the damage is not extensive. The dusk is seeping up Princes Avenue and seems a long way from the river. We go back to the Malay club, clean up and then go down to see our ship mates. We do not want to draw our knives. They have not hurt us but if we cut them, the police would come and we would be in the jail by the morning. To miss a ship is a serious business back then. We return to Granby Street in the early morning. It is like sixth and tenth in San Francisco or

Saint Catherine Street in Montreal with its cafes and clubs. They know us there. Those times stand with me when we address our own seamen, I should not have let them hit my friend. I should have done more.'

'Why don't you tell me of your other daughter,' I want to ask, 'the one with eyes that burn right through you and taken from a photograph you keep as solace within your prison. Why don't you mention her?' But I do not say a word.

The letter asks the Kalimantan woman to come and see Iskra if she has any feelings for him. The night is pulling away and I can see the moon above the harbour. The sky is clear, a good sign for the fishing and there are no trawlers in the river. They would lie heavy at the quayside by morning; hard work and another long day. I hoped Mo thinks of me somewhere behind his closed and darkened shutters.

Chapter Fourteen

Iskra and 'his woman'

Iskra calls me early on Saturday and says he's sent the letter. I had been to the movies twice with Mo that week. We couldn't be seen holding hands up and down the street for obvious reasons but it doesn't matter what you do inside, everybody knows that. Mo doesn't always understand what he sees on the screen, so I have to explain everything to him. When Iskra comes around it's just after seven in the morning. I had scrambled some time off. Mo came over last night as we'd arranged to go out to a tidal lake near the river. You have to be up early to go there and be back in the city for lunch. It is a beautiful spot, the water fringed with yellow grasses and beyond it, the grey green light of the Mangroves.

We take the bus and travel a few kilometres outside of Kuching to a place that nestles between rocks and is strung with wooden reeds along the inland side of the lake. The morning sun is very hot and the water's warm, carried by with long lazy waves, especially when a boat comes across. Mo teaches me a game. While we're swimming, we have to drink in the tops of the waves and gather all the foam we could into our mouths; then we have to turn over and float on our backs while spraying the water up towards the sky. The foam is frothy and disappears into the air or falls back onto my face like warm rain. After a while my mouth is burning from the bitter salt.

After we get dressed, Mo looks at me; his eyes are shining. We don't say anything. Id left my window open last night and it feels good to feel the summer night flowing over my body again. Dada does not talk to me today nor do I feel another's eyes upon me. Coming back, I tell Mo that we can have lunch together. I go downstairs to buy some meat. I hear a woman's voice coming from Ikra's room. It must be around noon because Srino can be heard shouting at his bird, the sound of footsteps, old Srino's voice and the bird crying and scratching as they go down the wooden stairs together , then, the usual curses, "Bastard, dirty swine" as they hit the street.

I tell Mo all about the old man and he laughs. He is wearing one of my pyjama tops with the sleeves rolled up. When he laughs, I wonder about out time together in Dada's house and all the other stuff I don't like to think about.

A moment later, Mo asks me if I love him. I tell him that doesn't mean anything around here, but I don't want to disappoint him. He looks sad then. But while we are making lunch he laughs again, for no apparent reason, and the way he laughs makes me laugh as well.

'Of course I do,' I say, which makes him laugh even more.

Just at that moment, we hear a fight break out in Iskra's place. First we hear the high pitched voice of a woman and then Iskra saying:

'You cheated on me, you humiliated me. I'll teach you to cheat on me.'

There are a few muffled sounds, followed by the woman screaming so horribly that in a flash everyone rushes out onto the landing. Mo and I also go out. The woman keeps screaming and Iskra keeps hitting her. Mo says this is awful. I don't reply but I think it is awful as well. He asks me to go and get a policeman but I tell him I don't like the police.

'Neither do I,' he says, 'but we need them now.'

But then one shows up with the plumber who lives on the second floor.

He knocks on the door and everything goes quiet inside. He bangs harder and, after a moment, the woman starts crying and Iskra opens the door. He is smoking a cigarette and looks as if he has just eaten a heavy lunch. Stubble is gathered on his face and he looks slightly red eyed. The young woman rushes to the door and tells the policeman that Iskra has beaten her. 'Name,' says the cop, 'and take that cigarette out of your mouth when you're talking to me.' Iskra hesitates, glances over at me and takes another drag of his cigarette. When he does that, the policeman, in his freshly pressed blue shirt slaps him so hard across the face that you could hear it across the landing. His cigarette goes flying.

Iskra turns pale and you can see his eyes dance but he doesn't say anything. He then meekly asks if he can pick up his cigarette. The Cop says said he can but adds, 'Next time, you remember; only fools or tourists take us for idiots in Malaysia.' While this is going on, the young woman keeps crying and says:

'He hit me. He's a pimp,' over and over again.

Then Iskra says, 'Tell me, officer, isn't it against the laws of this country to call a man a pimp?' But the policeman only replies: 'Shut your trap.'

Iskra turns to the girl and says: 'You haven't seen the last of me.'

The policeman tells him to shut up again and says that the girl should leave and that Iskra should stay put until he's told to come down to the police station. He adds that Iskra should be ashamed of himself that he's shaking so much.

'Are you drunk?' the policeman asks. A little gasp goes up from the people on the landing. The Government says drink is the curse of our Nation, especially here in Kuching.

Iskra says, 'I'm not drunk, officer. It's just that I am standing in front of you and all these people, and of course I'm shaking. It is my shame, I cannot help it.'

He closes the door and everyone leaves. Mo and I finish making lunch but his appetite has gone. He keeps looking at Iskra's door with frightened eyes. I eat nearly all of it. He goes at two o'clock and I sleep for a little while.

Around an hour later, Iskra knocks on my door. I am still lying down. He sits on the edge of the bed. He doesn't say anything at first and I ask him how it has gone. He tells me he has done what he has planned but then she slaps him across the face and so he started hitting her back.

'You've seen what happens next.' he says.

I tell him that it seems to me that she has been punished and that he should be satisfied.

'That's also my opinion,' Iskra says.

He points out that it doesn't matter what the police-man has done because it wouldn't change the fact that he's given her a good beating. Then he adds he knows what cops are like and just how to deal with them. He asks me if I had any different opinion at all.

'Nothing,' I say and besides, 'I don't like the police.' Iskra seems pleased.

He asks me if I want to go out somewhere with him.

I get up and comb my hair. He tells me that I have to act as a witness for him. As far as I am concerned, it doesn't bother me in the least but I don't know what he wants me to say.

According to Iskra, all I have to say is that the girl has cheated on him. I agree to stand. We go to a bar and Iskra buys me a brandy and ginger. Then he wants to play pool and I nearly beat him. Afterwards, he asks me to go to a brothel but I say no because I don't like that kind of thing. We walk slowly back home and he tells me how happy he is that he's managed to pun-ish his mistress without doing what the gangsters have suggested or having to go to them for favours. He's being very kind to me and I think this is a good mo-ment, cool under the branches with the Mengaris trees flowering in gold along the river and the mosque and churches and shrines glinting in the last of the sun. Iskra seems very close to me.

In the distance, I notice Srino standing at the doorway. He is looking upset. When we get closer, I see that his bird is no longer in the cage. He's looking every-where, turning round in circles and trying to see inside the dark hallway. He mumbles incoherently and then peers up in the air or down the street with his little red eyes. When Iskra asks him what's wrong, he doesn't answer right away. I can just about make out what he's saying – 'Bastard, dirty swine.' – and then getting all worked up. I ask him about his parrot.

'The bastard's escaped.' he answers me sharply. 'He's flown away. God knows where it has got the strength from.' Then suddenly, he starts to talk very quickly:

'I took him to the waterfront, as usual. The crowds gather down there because of the fair stalls. I stop to have a look at the one of the escape artists. Going to leave, I go to close his cage but the bastard's gone. Of course, I'd been meaning to close the door for such a long time. But I never wanted to believe that dirty swine could fly away like that.'

'Do you think that anyone understands what goes on in front of them?' Iskra asks.

He says that the bird must have got lost and then he'd come back. He gives Srino lots of examples of birds that have travelled hundreds of miles to make their way back home.

'They're the same as people,' he says, 'they always come back.'

In spite of that, the old man seems even more upset. 'The bastard can't walk let alone fly but they'll still take him away from me, don't you understand? It wouldn't be so bad if I thought someone might take him in. But that's impossible; he disgusts everyone with his scabby plumage. If the police pick him up, they'll destroy him as a health risk.'

I tell him that all he has to do is go down to the police's lost property and make a gentle enquiry. He'll get the bird back if he pays enough of a fee. He asks me if the fee is very expensive, I say I don't know. Then he gets angry. 'Pay good money for that scabby bastard. He can go to hell!' he starts cursing him. Iskra shakes his head and laughs and goes inside the house. I follow him in and we say goodbye on the landing. A moment later, I hear the old man's footsteps and he knocks on my door. When I open it, he stands there for a moment then finally says: 'I'm sorry.'

I ask him if he wants to step inside. At first he says no but very quickly and sounding rather embarrassed he says he knows people in the neighbourhood that thought badly of me because of my Dada and that my mother and father are right to do what they do in order to keep me straight. He says that it is good that Dada has died up there in that home alone, because that way he can't be seen to betray any more people nor his stigma run like a stain across our family.

'I know you loved the Dada a lot,' he says.

I reply that I haven't been aware people had criticized me about that, but letting Dada go back to that village has been the best choice I could give him, it gives him his chance to make peace and it seems the natural thing to do.

'I looked after him long enough,' I say.

'I don't earn enough to take care of him and the home is part of his entitlement to his seaman's pension.

'And besides,'; I add, 'For a long time he doesn't have anything to talk to me about, and then he can't stop and he wears me out ,especially when I start to change everything in my life. He gets bored by himself after that.'

'Yes,' old Srino says, 'and at least back in the village he knows people.'

Then he said he'd be going.

He wants to go to his bed. His life has changed now and he doesn't quite know how to prepare for it. For the first time since I'd come to live here, he shyly offers me his hand. When I shake it I can feel the scales of his skin. He gives me a little smile as he leaves and says, 'Hope the birds don't sing too early in the morning. I always think that one of them is mine even if he can only hop about and mouth obscenities. I should never have given him his freedom. What will he do, what he will do?' he suddenly wails. Iskra hasn't closed his door. He is silhouetted, a dark lumpy shape, against the frame. He takes the last of the air. He shakes his head.

'Your Dada would have laughed,' he says.

Does he know Dada's secret as well? How his mother is raped by a good Christian, a great nephew of the Sultan White Rajah; his surrogate father, an estate manager and Buddhist Chinese who rears him and gets him away to sea or that his own wife and daughter, so fierce in their desire for Islam, leave him for Singapore?

Iskra says. 'Another girl lived here.'

I think of this when I smell the wind and see the stars. Does one of them shine for her, the other daughter? They look down as if they are weeping. Do they think I am looking for the Dada or they weeping for me?

'She is about ten years older.' Iskra says.

It comes to me with a sudden clarity that Dada could not know all the things he tells me. Someone must have let him in on it. He could not have imagined all the times that brought him to this moment as he docks from one port to another in the service of the Blue Funnel Line or of his own mother a sea Dayak won as a prize.

Is it his adopted father who tells him in his bitterness of the mother's early death, the responsibility thrown upon his shoulders for the adopted son? The revenge that brings the Dada to rebel against the State at the very moment of its own shaky foundation, is it the same bitterness that my father chews upon when he informs me of his secret? Maybe the strike of all the Borneo seamen comes at just at the wrong time, the same as my father's bile when he sees spies around every corner. It's difficult to know these things, what rage, what responsibility?

I say goodnight to Iskra.

'Goodnight my friend.' he says, 'Never forget those who treat you with disdain.'

Chapter Fifteen

The Lady in Blue - a baby passed over

Iskra phones me next morning at the dock office. I can see him now with his forearms and boxer's nose. He says that one of his friends, he's told him about me, has invited us to spend Sunday at his beach house near the port. I say I'd like that very much but I'd promised to spend the day with Mo. Iskra immediately says, he's invited as well. His friend's wife would be very happy not to be between men. She might have a friend over herself. He chuckles.

'She says she knows someone who knows you,' he says.

I want to hang up right away because I find myself confused. I know that my boss doesn't like us getting personal calls when we're at work.

Iskra asks me to hold on a moment. He says he could have told me about the invitation this evening but he wants to warn me about something. It's the brother of his former mistress and a group of his Kalimantan friends who have been following him all day.

'If you see him near the house tonight when you get home, let me know,' he says.

I said that I would. A little while later, my boss asks to see me. I am annoyed at first because I think he's going to tell me I should spend less time talking on the phone and more time working.

But it's not about that at all. He says he wants to speak to me about a project that is still in the planning stages and that he wants my opinion on the matter.

He is thinking of setting up an office on the mainland, in the capital, where they could really deal directly with the large companies they did business with there and where many of the international shipping lines are based.

'You studied before you let everything go and came to work here,' he says.

He wants to know if I'd be interested in going over there to work. It would mean I could live in Kuala Lumpur and also travel part of the year all over Australasia studying the transportation and logistics of the fishing business.

'It's a very dynamic industry,' he says. 'You're young and it seems to me it might be the kind of life you'd enjoy?'

I say 'Yes that's true, but I actually, don't care one way or the other. I like it around here. I am a Dayak and this is my home.'

'With our borders, it's the same as being in a different country,' I say.

He asks me if I'm not interested in changing my life. I reply that you can never really change your life and that, in any case, every life is more or less that same and my life here is not all that bad once you know who you are. He doesn't look pleased and tells me I can never give a straight answer to anything.

'You have no ambition and that is disastrous in business, especially one so quickly changing as this industry where quota stocks move fast from year to year even across this island, not to say all the others on the greater and lesser Sundaes.'

I carry on working. I say nothing. Silence generally works. I do not want to upset him, but I can see no reason to change my life. Anyone who gives it serious thought always knows it can be different but why? As a student, I had great ambitions about having a career especially to please my father but when he chooses to tell me about this business of Dada's secret, I don't want to continue with my studies. I soon realize that none of that sort of stuff matters very much especially when you talk about identity; what it means to have it taken away and what it is to find it. Pirates do not care about stuff like this. They have no country only place. They are in between people, not like those who live on the land and measure their days by the sun.

That evening, Mo comes to see me. He says that we can get together if I want. He asks me if I want him to move in, to live together with him. I reply that it's no big deal and doesn't mean that much but I say sure. The house is empty now with Dada gone. It would be good to share. Mo goes to protest. I say, don't worry of course, I'm joking. And besides, if he asks me nicely I'd be happy to say yes. He says that living together is a serious business especially in this country.

I say: 'Not at all! You just have do what everyone else does here; keep quiet and fake it. Then they leave you alone. You told me that,' I say

He says nothing. For a moment he just looks at me

in silence; then he says he simply wants to know if I would say yes to any other man who asks me.

'Probably,' I say.

He wonders if I really love him but no way can I know anything about that. After a moment's silence, he murmurs that I'm very strange. He undoubtedly loves me for that very reason, but then one day he might find me repulsive, for that very same reason if I do something he finds outrageous. When I say nothing, because I have nothing more to say, he smiles. He puts his arm through mine and says he wants us to get together and we should celebrate this weekend. He says we can do it as soon as we want. I tell him about my boss's plan and he says he'd like to get to know Kuala Lumpur and that whole Australasian thing. I tell him I have no big plans, except for sailing a fast pirate ship around all the islands.

'It's easy for you,' he says.

'Dangerous,' I say 'but easy as well.'

I tell him we have been invited down to the beach with Iskra this Sunday. Mo claps his hands.

'Oh yes, that will be our celebration,' he says.

That evening we go for a walk along the wide avenues that lead to the waterfront. The men we see are all beautiful and I ask Mo if he notices that. He says he has and that he understands me but to be careful with my words and what I say because it can affect others.

For a while, we don't speak. I want him to stay with me, though, and I tell him we can eat together at Jalima's. He says he'd really like to, but he has other things to do.

We are nearly back at my place. I say goodbye to him. He looks at me: 'Don't you want to know what I have to do?' he says.

I do want to know, but I haven't said which is why he seemed to be reproaching me. Then, when he sees me getting tied up in knots trying to explain, he laughs again and leans his head towards mine so I can kiss him. We pull each other to the shadows.

'I have to get ready to move house,' he says.

'I'm finished with that old has been,' he whispers.

I order a fish and noodle soup, the speciality at Jalima's. I had already started eating when a strange little woman in a blue suit comes into the café. She moves to the other side of the room. Jalima is busy and she asks if the woman can share my table but I shake my head. She comes over anyway and parks herself down. She calls out even though she's less than a metre away and says she knows me and has seen me with the Dada. She has sharp, jerky gestures and bright eyes in a small round face. Her eyes bear into me as she fiddles with her earrings and the jewellery on her fingers. She takes off her jacket and stares busily at the menu. She calls Jalima over and immediately orders what she wants in a hurried but very precise tone of voice. While waiting for her first course, she opens her bag and takes out a little notebook and a pencil.

'I've been following you. I know your Dada. Do you know why I wear blue?' she shouts.

She adds up what her bill would come to, then takes out her purse and places enough money to cover the exact amount, including the tip, on the table in front of her. Just then, her first course arrives, which she wolfs down very quickly.

'I wear blue because it symbolises the mixture of our blood,' she says.

'Our Lady wore blue do you know that? Do you know your Dada was devoted to our blessed mother even though they called him a communist and made him sick with the divisions on this island?'

'Pure blood,' she snorts, 'who has got that around here?'

I continue with my soup. When she's shouting, she reminds me of Dada.

'We are all of us of the mix,' she says. I look up.

'I know what you're like on the inside,' she says.

I nod and stir my noodles and marinated fish. I think she's crazy.

'Remember what I tell you' she says. I nod again the way I always do when I want things to be quiet, just to keep her quiet.

While waiting for the next course, she takes a magazine out of her large bag. The glossy pages list the week's satellite television. Very carefully, she places a tick beside almost every programme, one by one. Since the magazine contains about twelve pages, she continues her meticulous work throughout the entire meal.

'This is how they sell us pictures and tell us who we are,' she says.

I have finished eating but she frowns, still totally engrossed in making her notes. Then she stands up, puts her jacket on with the precise movements of a bird and makes to leave.

She gives a pursed little smile and her eyes dance as she moves away from the table.

'If you follow me I'll tell you something,' she says.

Since Mo has gone to his old lover's I wait a moment then follow her. She walks to the edge of the pavement with a little crabbed movement and heads up the road towards the bus station near to the water. She walks in a straight line without looking back. Her movements are so precise and fast that it looks as if she might rise up off the pavements and fly like some little bird but not high enough or low enough to avoid disaster. I think of old Srino's parrot. I can see my mother in her somehow. How was I to know she would preside as the companion to that unhappy woman at the closing stages of my life?

Eventually, I lose sight of her and I turn around and think to walk back home. She is very strange and I would soon forget her but she intrigues me.

'A baby lost is a baby passed over,' she appears beside me.

Old Srino is standing in front of my door. I show him in and he tells me that his bird has stayed missing this time and is not at the sanctuary. The employees there have told him that the bird has perhaps been taken. He asks if he can find out for sure at the police station but they tell him that they don't keep records because such things happen every day.

I say to him that he can get another bird, but he says he's used to this one. I sit on the edge of my bed and Srino sits facing me on a chair by the table.

He has his hands on his knees. He keeps hold of his cap. It is hard to understand him because he is mumbling beneath his yellowish moustache.

He bores me with this story but I have so many things circling around in my head and as I'm not tired and just to say something, I ask him about his bird. He tells me he'd got him after his wife died.

He married rather late in life. When he was young, he

wanted to work in the theatre, while his dad spent time in the army when the British were on the peninsula. The white Rajahs still rule all this part of Borneo up to then. He acts in vaudeville to entertain the troops when the troubles start with the Chinese planters in the jungle.

He ends up working on the railways over there but he had no regrets because it's a good job that his dad had helped him with and he now has a small pension. He hadn't been happy with his wife but in the end he'd got used to living with her as well.

When she died, he felt very lonely. So he asked one of his workmates what could he do for company and they had bought him a bird in a cage. He had got the parrot when it was still very young and fresh from the jungle. He had to feed it with a baby's bottle. But since birds like that can live to an old age and they mature very quickly they'd ended up growing old together.

'He was bad tempered bastard.': old Srino told me. 'From time to time, we'd have it out. But goodness came out of him just the same.'

'He's a good breed,' I say and Srino seems pleased.

'And you didn't even know him before he got sick,' he adds. 'His plumage used to be the most beautiful thing about him like a horse chestnut tree in flower.' Every morning and every evening after the bird got skin disease, Srino rubs him gently with oil under his wing feathers.

'But,' he said, 'his real disease is old age, and no one can cure that.'

I yawn just then and the old man says he has to go.

I tell him he can stay and that I'm sorry about what has happened to his bird. He thanks me. He tells me that

Dada also liked the parrot. When he mentions him, he calls him 'Your poor father.'

He hints that I must be very unhappy since Dada has died, but I don't reply or even try to correct him that Dada is my Grandfather and more to me than to any of those who disown him.

He says, 'You're a good kid, but you're strange and you mix with strange people. Let me give you some advice, stay away from that Iskra character. He knows more than his bones. We don't need any more disturbances around here. He'll get you into trouble.'

He raises a make-believe pipe into the air and swivels his eyes. It makes me laugh to see the old man like that. It must have been a trick from his entertaining days. We finish on a good note and he says goodnight. I lean back and feel the whole of Borneo burst out its breath beneath me like a hoary old wolf or sea rat. The call of a yellow beaked hornbill echoes out over the water and brings together all our unhappy histories. The eyes of the woman in blue shine out at me; as bright as the orchids that flower out of season, eyes in the photograph they give me from the home upriver, wrapped in the rest of Dada's meagre belongings.

Chapter Sixteen

The Beach House

Sunday, I find it difficult to wake, still half dreaming, half sleeping, Mo calls my name and shakes me. They are burning wood in Kalimantan. We don't eat because we want to go for a swim. I feel completely empty, desolate, hollowed out and my heads hurt. My cigarette tastes bitter. Mo makes fun of me.

'You look like death,' he says.

He wears a white suit and has left his hair down. I tell him he's beautiful and it would be better if we are not all mixed up like snails in a sack across all the borders and districts of this island. He laughs and sounds pleased. He always misses the beat. On the way out we knock on Iskra's door. Wood smoke crosses the whole island and almost drowns the hills with the smell of that fucking crew. The poor will burn anything. You don't need logging companies to ruin a forest. Two weeks have gone by since Dada's death.

I'm tired and because last night we'd kept the shutters closed the air feels like a slap across my face; an irritation that confuses me, between stuff that I know and what I don't. Mo is really excited to be going to the beach and keeps on saying what a beautiful day it is and we would soon be serene. I start to feel a bit better. I realize I'm hungry. I say this to Mo and he points to the market where I work. I make to put a finger down my throat. He laughs.

I would have to wait. We hear Iskra close his door and his steps coming down to the street.

He is wearing blue trousers and an expensive short sleeved white shirt. He's put on a baseball cap which makes Mo laugh. His skin is very pale under the dark hair on his thick forearms. His father would never have got into the engine room of the Blue Funnel Line like Dada.

I find him a little repulsive. He is whistling as he comes down the stairs and looks happy. He says, 'Hello my special men,' to Mo and me and calls us 'his little gangsters.' The day before, I had gone to the police station and given my statement, saying that his Indonesian woman had been 'disrespectful' towards him. He gets off with a warning but they slap him around a bit when he offers them money.

No one has any problem with my statement. While we are standing by the door, we talk about 'his crime.' We then decide to take the car to the rocks. The beach isn't far but we'd get there faster that way instead of waiting around for a bus. Iskra thinks his friend will be pleased if we get there early. We're just about to leave when he suddenly gestures for me to look across the street. A group of 'Mantans are leaning against the window of the tobacco shop. They are watching us in silence, but in a way that is particular to them; looking through us as if we are stones or dead trees.

Iskra says that the guy second from left is the girl's brother, the one that he's been telling me about. He seems worried but then he adds that it's all ancient history now. Mo doesn't understand what is going on and asks us what's wrong. I tell him they're immigrant Indos who have a grudge against Iskra.

Mo wants us to leave right away. Iskra stands up tall and laughs and says we'd better hurry up. We get to the car and Iskra asks if they are following us. I turn around. They haven't moved but just keep staring at the same spot with the same air of indifference, the girl's brother wears a flowered shirt.

Iskra seems relieved when we get going. He tells us one joke after another. I have a feeling he's attracted to Mo. Mo barely says a word to him but every now and again he would look at him and his eyes have a strange something about them.

Typical Sarawak I think, fucking Borneo, where no one looks at each other and when they do it's either to put you down or tug at your number between sex and nation. It is little wonder the Dayaks rebel or want no part of it.

We pass Damai, one of the main beach resorts on the Santubong Peninsula. We have been driving for just over half an hour. I feel sick again. The area has sandy beaches at the foot of the jungle-covered mountains but we don't want to see the world-class resort hotels like the Damai Beach Resort, or the Damai Puri Spa or the One Hotel. We don't need their private beaches, swimming pools or Jet Skis, water-skiing, windsurfing or mountain biking. Squash and fitness centres mean nothing to us. Nor are we attracted by the international standard 18-hole golf course designed by Arnold Palmer. Who the fuck is Arnie to us? We are going to Lundu Beach with its rocky pebbles and rough sand where you can see the port and it's nice to know where our drugs come in on freighters close to Sematan. Iskra is driving slow, taking his time.

We get out beyond the suburbs. The beach isn't far from the car park by the docks. We have to walk across a little ridge that looks out to the sea and then drops steeply down to the shore. It is coloured in yellowish rocks and white daisies that stand out sharply against the relentless clouding and unfolding of the sky. The rain is coming back. All dead flowers rise again here especially with the constant rain. Mo thinks it fun to scatter their petals by making low sweeps at them with his bag. We walk through rows of little houses with green or white fences; some of them have verandas and are hidden by tamarisk and yellow pineapple bushes while others stand stark and lifeless amid the rocks in the lemon light.

Before reaching the edge of the ridge, we can already make out the still water that leads from the South China Sea to Sulawesi and closer in, an enormous deserted promontory where they used to hang fishing nets across the tidal flow. We can hear the distant sound of a motor through the quiet air. Then we see a little trawler in the distance, inching its way towards us over the purple and luminous water.

'Fucking Thai cunts,' Iskra says.

I look away. Surrounding the mouth of the river are the forests that rise away on both banks. Fig trees cling to them and you can see where the red fruit has dropped into the water. To get stuck in there would be worse than any maze. To search for exotic flowers might be interesting for an anthropologist but what if you got trapped? People do get lost and die. A quarter of a century ago my father could not wait to get away from his jungle village. He wants to work in the city and live in the suburbs. Dada used to say the only people who die in the jungle are tourists; those who work in them are too busy making a living.

'Are we like that little ship heading for our own rocks?' Mo says.

'Do you mean getting stupid?' Iskra laughs. He means our crystal ice and the weed we roll as a chaser to the amphetamine. I laugh as well but it is a tired one.

From the steep slope leading down towards the sea, we can see that a few people are already in the water. Iskra's friend lives in what looks like a wooden hut on stilts at the other end of the promontory. There is a small little space out on the back deck where they used to gut the fish. The house is near the rocks but its supports at the front are already below the water level, rickety stairs lead up to the living quarters. Iskra introduces us. His friend is called Shabela.

He is a tall man, enormous, with very broad shoulders and a big stomach. He tells us to make ourselves at home and says that they are frying fish they'd caught that very morning. I tell him how great I think his house is and he says that he spends every Saturday and Sunday and every day he has off down here.

'My wife gets on very well with people and has lots of friends;' he adds.

Just then, perhaps because I realize I'm going to get strung out again, I think of how strangely the way of my life has changed. It is when these sudden surges of energy run through me at the closeness of the water that the first thoughts come to me that I can live like a pirate, like my ancient people. I could hold fast while the wind would catch my sails and take me cleaving all the way up and down the Malay Peninsula. Shabela might have been a captain like Loh Seh the great Chinese robber who ran a hundred ships with her captains as her lovers but he is Malay like Iskra and has forgotten his history. Mine rubs against me like the jagged rocks. Shabela wants to go swimming. His wife and Iskra don't want to come along.

'We have things to talk about,' he says.

The three of us go down to the beach and Mo jumps straight into the water.

Shabela and I wait a bit. He speaks slowly and I notice he has the habit of ending everything he says with 'and of the blessings of God,' even when he is actually adding nothing that changes the meaning of what he's already said. Mo says about his wife,

'She's terrific and of the blessings of God.'

It's a joke but Shabela doesn't see it. I stop paying attention to his little mannerism because I'm thinking about how wonderful it is to be out in the sun, how the clouds are shifting and even if it is not long before the rain comes down in the purple laden blankets, it doesn't matter. Even the rocks are warm under my feet. Despite my eagerness to get into the water, I resist for a while longer but Shabela finally says 'Ready?' and I dive in. Shabela walks slowly into the water and only starts swimming when it is deep around his waist. He's doing the breaststroke, and rather badly, so I leave him on his own and go to join Mo.

The water is warm and I am happy to be swimming. Mo

and I swim far out, moving in harmony with each other; I'm glad to be away from the atmosphere of Dada's death and thoughts of my own father's corrective life.

Once we are out in open water, we float on our backs and I gaze up at the sky; the sun dries away the last of the water that trickles down my face into my mouth. We see that Shabela has gone back near the rocks to stretch out beneath the sun. Even from a distance, he looks enormous. Mo wants us to swim together. I get behind him so I can hold him around the waist and he swims forward using his arms while I help him by kicking my legs. The gentle sound of the splashing water in the yellow morning light stays with us for some time until I get tired and the bitter taste in my mouth reminds me of how I woke up. I leave Mo where he is treading water and swim back at normal pace, taking deep breaths. I stretch out on my stomach on the beach near Shabela and rest my head on the sand.

I tell him 'This feels good,' and he agrees.

'Love always feels good,' he says, 'and of the blessing of god.'

A little while later, Mo comes out of the water. I turn around to watch him walk towards us. He is covered in a film of salt and is holding his hair back. He lies down, gently pressing against me while pretending to look away. The heat from our two bodies and the sun behind the clouds makes me feel drowsy and I doze. Mo gives me a shake and tells me that Shabela has gone back to the house because it's time for lunch. I get up right away. I'm hungry. Mo whispers that I haven't kissed him all morning. That is true, but we have to be careful.

'Come into the water,' he says.

We run and splash through the shallow little waves. We swim for a while and then he presses his body against mine. I feel his legs wrap around me and I want him the same as I wanted him last night beneath the window with the ratchets of light that are caught between the closed shutters and the moving shadows of the street. When we come out of the water, Shabela's already calling us. I say I'm very hungry, and right away he tells me his wife says she likes me.

'She's from Singapore,' Shabela says.

'I have a surprise for you,' his wife says, 'just you wait.' The food is good. I wolf down my bread and fish. Then we have some beef and fried potatoes. We all sat in silence. Shabela drinks a lot of juice and keeps filling up my glass. By the time we are having coffee, my head feels heavy. I'd smoked a lot of cigarettes and what I hadn't smoked we'd rolled.

Shabel, Iskra and I talk about how we might spend the month of August together at the beach and sharing the expenses.

Suddenly Mo says 'Do you know what time it is, it's only twelve thirty.'

We are surprised, but Shabela says 'You can never eat too early, it's only natural, and the time to eat is when you're hungry.'

I don't know why that makes me laugh but I find it difficult to stop. Shabela asks me if I want to go for a walk on the beach with him.

'My wife always takes a nap after lunch. But I don't like to, I need a walk. I keep telling her it's healthier. But in the end, it's up to her.'

Just then, his wife is joined at the house by the woman in blue. She looks directly at me. In my bones I somehow know this is meant to happen. This is my surprise. She is dressed entirely in that one colour broken only by strips of silver. She peers at me closely like she did in the restaurant, as if she has known me all her life.

'I am a gatherer of stories,' she says.

'And you also tell lies,' I say.

She wears the same series of little silver encased jewels about her body.

'Why would I lie about your poor Dada?' she says.

'You'll come to a bad end if you don't change,' she says again suddenly.

'I'm with my friends. Shut your mouth.' I say.

'Come around to the back and I'll tell you something,' she says.

She fumbles in her bag as if searching for a paper to give me but seems to forget it and instead searches me again with her face as if something has gone missing.

'It's natural to protect your family even to those born wrong,' she says.

I raise my hand to slap her.

Shabela's wife pulls me to one side.

'Please don't treat her like that. She appears tough but she's very fragile,' she says.

'How do you know her?' I ask.

'She knows me from Singapore. She lived there for many years with her mother,

'They know how to live together there,' she says.

I shrug my shoulders and do not ask why. The woman in blue has crept back into the house.

'Now she stays alone in one of the villages up the river.' Shabela's wife says. 'She lives on her father's pension.'

Mo comes out. He looks embarrassed. He says he'll stay and help Shabela's wife with the dishes.

Shabela's wife turns around and says we men have to leave. She, her friend in blue and 'the little kitten' she calls Mo will clear up the dishes. The three of us go out onto the beach, Iskra, Shabela and myself.

The smallest clouds have cleared and the sun is beating down on the sand; its brilliance like glass off the water is almost unbearable. The beach is deserted now. We can hear the clinking sound of cutlery and dishes from the little houses along the sandstone ridge.

The heat rising from the rocks into the air makes it almost difficult to breath. At first Iskra and Shabela talk about things and people I don't know. I realized they've known each other for a long time and had even shared a place for a while.

'I've seen that woman around for years without even knowing her name,' Shabela laughs.

'She lived in our building at one time.' Iskra says.

We head towards the sea and walk along the water's edge. Every now and then a little wave that is longer than the last one wets our shoes and again my mind becomes blank because the heat on my bare head is making me feel drowsy. Shabela and Iskra both wear caps when walking. I seem to be labouring as if I'm trying to swim through the air.

Just then Iskra says something quick to Shabela that I can't make out. At the same time, I notice two Kalimantans, one wearing the yellow flowered shirt and the other in blue workman's overalls, coming towards us.

They are at the other end of the beach, still quite far away. I look at Iskra and he says;

'It's him again.'

We carry on walking. Shabela asks how they manage to follow us all the way here. I realize they must have got on the bus after seeing our beach bags loaded into Iskra's car, but I don't say anything. Even though they seem to move slowly, they're a lot closer to us now. We walk at the same pace, Iskra says to Shabela;

'If there's a fight, you take the second one, I'll take care of mine. If another one shows up, he's yours.' He stares at me.

I say 'Ok.'

Shabela looks swollen over the rock of his protruding stomach. Hair is matted down his strong legs. He looks very black. We walk steadily forward towards them. The rocks and pebbles are becoming more numerous under our feet and they are getting closer and closer, until they stay just a few steps away. Then they stop and I slow down. Iskra walks straight up to his man. I can't make out what they are saying. I am soaking, sweating with weed, with food, and the heat of the sky like a damp cloth has been held tightly to my forehead. One of the Kalimantans suddenly makes a menacing gesture as if he is going to punch Iskra in the face but Iskra hits him first and immediately calls out for Shabela who goes over to the second one and hits him twice with all his strength. The Indo falls face down into the water and stays there for a few seconds, little bubbles rise to the surface around his head. Meanwhile, Iskra has hit the other one again whose face is covered in blood.

He turns to me and says: 'Just you watch what I'm going to do to him.'

I shout: 'Look out, he's got a knife!' But by then, Iskra's arm is already cut and his mouth slashed.

Shabela leaps forward but the other one gets up and is standing beside his friend with the blade pointed quietly in our direction. We don't move. They walk slowly backwards, staring at us, keeping us at a distance by wielding the knife from side to side. When they see there is enough space between us, they run away very quickly. We remain pinned there under the coming rain that suddenly starts to pour. Steam rises from the rocks like from a pan of water.

Iskra is holding his arm that drips with blood. Shabela immediately tells us there is a doctor on the Ridge who spends every Sunday there. Shabela wants to go to see him right away. Every time Iskra tries to speak, blood from the gash in his mouth forms a little stream of spittle that runs down the side of his bottom lip. We hold him up and go back to the house as quickly as possible. When we get there, Iskra says his injuries are superficial but that he'll go and see the doctor anyway. He leaves with Shabela and I stay behind with Mo to explain what has happened. Shabela's wife starts crying and Mo starts to cry as well, but I tell them to fucking well shut up. They are as bad as old Srino and his missing bird. The woman in blue says nothing.

The thought distracts me as I look out over the sea and listen to the occasional choking sob coming from the house.

She appears in the doorway.

'You can't escape anything when chance forces itself upon you,' she says.

I look at her. 'Don't tell me my fortune,' I say.

'I can tell you the truth,' she says. 'When a baby is passed over, a child is lost.'

Chapter Seventeen

They call me Sea Dayak

It annoys me to have to explain everything over and again to Mo and Shabela's wife.

'My little friend is leaving,' she says.

The woman in blue appears at the top of the wooden stairs.

'I wouldn't speak of your Dada before when they were putting him in jail or keeping him at the house, but now he's dead, it's different,' she says.

'God rest his soul. It's different. He's done his penance in time for the world to know what it's like to be a Sea Dayak in this fugitive territory.'

I don't say a thing. I imagine Srino's missing bird flying over the water, too high or too low with its oiled wings cheating disease or death until the sun would rise higher and consume him like the labyrinth, only another word for what toils within us on this island. 'It's what's inside you that counts,' she says.

She reminds me of a little Myna bird that fights to roll and sing its way through life. Her mouth rises and falls as the stories cascade out of her in little hurried starts. The explosion is over as sudden as it has begun. She looks exhausted as if she is already beyond her time. Her face sags and her eyes seem to sink deeper into her skin.

'Your Dada is my father,' she ends quietly.

I watch her fly away across the foreshore with her tiny furious steps. Her shoulders seem to heave.

At about four-thirty, Iskra comes back with Shabela. His arm is bandaged and he has a patch over the corner of his mouth. He's trying hard to smile if you could call it that.

The doctor has told him it is superficial but he still looks pretty gloomy. Shabela tries to make him laugh but he refuses to say anything. When he says he's going back down to the rocks, I ask him where he's heading.

'Fuck off,' he says.

A little calmer he replies that he wants to get some cooler air. Shabela and I say we'll go with him but then he gets angry again and swears at us. Shabela says it's best not to upset him but I follow him anyway. We walk along the beach for a long while. The rain is beating down. Its force crashes and scatters the sand into little pockets like bullets ripping away across the foreshore and peppering the sea. I have the impression that Iskra knows where he's going but I say nothing. Shabela stays at home and with the blessing of god.

At the very end of the beach, we come to a little hut. Behind it a stream flows down into the sand from behind the large outcropped rock shelter where swimmers used to change. It's there that we see the two Kalimantans again. They are stretched out by the corners of the stone. They look calm and almost pleased.

Our presence doesn't seem to bother them and their expressions don't change.

The brother of the girl who'd attacked Iskra looks at him in silence. The other one is blowing into a little harmonica, playing the same three notes over and over again, while watching us from out the corner of his eye. All this time there is nothing but the splat splat of the rain on the bitumen roof and the silence, a hooter from an occasional passing ship, the soft sound of the flowing water and the musical notes from the silent host.

Iskra takes a knife out from his pocket. The Kalimantans don't move. They keep tight to each other. I notice that the one playing the harmonica is bent on one knee and has spread his toes out very wide as if in a kneeling crouch, the way you see anyone who works in confined conditions.

Without taking his eyes off his enemy, Iskra asks me: 'Shall I kill him?' I think that if I say no, he'll get all worked up again and will certainly do it.

'He hasn't said a word to you yet. It wouldn't be right to stab him like that,' I say.

We can hear the soft harmonica notes against the rain and the deep silence.

Iskra says, 'all right then; I'll swear at him and when he answers back, I'll stab him.'

I reply: 'Right. But if he doesn't take out his knife you can't stab him first.'

Iskra starts getting all worked up. The other one keeps playing his tune and both of them are staring at us, watching every movement.

'No.' I say. 'Take him on man to man and give me the knife. If the other one joins in or he pulls out his blade, I'll go for him.'

Iskra gives me his weapon. The rain drips in silver drops off the end of it. I can smell his sweat and the essence of orchid and oleander that he used as cologne. It is like the smell of the plants raised on my Dada's balcony, all reds and greens and yellows. It is around this time that he starts to get weak and to look at me with a strange glaze in his eyes. He leaves for the home upriver soon after.

We stand still, as if everything is closing in around us. We are staring at each other and everything stops, caught between the sea, the rain, the river and unusual silence of the water. At that very moment, I think about giving the knife back to Iskra but suddenly, the Kalimantans inch along the wall and scuttle away from us. They hide behind the outcrop.

When I go close, I see the one with the harmonica has left the scene. The girl's brother in the flowered shirt is alone stretched out on his back, his hands under his neck, his forehead hidden in shadow; his whole body seems loosened by the clouds that suck in the heat. His clothes are steaming. I'm a little surprised. As far as I am concerned, the matter is closed and it's just by chance I have ended up here. As soon as he sees me, he raises himself up and puts his hand to his pocket. I instinctively feel for Iskra's knife. Then he leans away again but keeps his hand near to his jeans. I am quite far away from him, about five metres or so but I can see him looking at me. Every now and then, his eyes close. But most of the time his face seems to flicker before me like a charred light within a stack of embers, the face of a religion, with the air rising and falling around him in a life of its own.

The sound of waves is more restless than the languorous calm of midday as the tide begins to turn. It is the same relentless heat but without sun, a heat that chills you; a watery yellow light that shines periodically across this island.

I do not stop watching the Kalimantan but something breaks inside me. Those things I never like to talk about dance around me now. I think about the rivers and seas that connect our island and the sound of the rattan lash within our house and I hear my own cries above my father's bitter sentiment.

'For over a thousand years the Chinese have poured over the Sunda and you say the world has misunderstood the lives of the Sea Dayaks. They accommodate them. I say we must maintain our Malay identity. It is the only promise left to us.'

'Everything is eaten or beaten here,' the Dada used to say.

His laugh would brighten a room, as great as the stars in heaven or grains of sand on the shore. I am not afraid of the Indonesians. Some might say they are only poor immigrants but I would have killed them if they moved against us. The girl's brother in his flowered shirt melts away into the silence.

No sun hovers in the sky now, only two hours since it has cast anchor in an ocean of molten metal. On the tide container ships start to move away from the port. Towards the horizon the small cargo boat passes on its way and I can see its dark smudge across the South China Sea.

'Do the deal with Shabela and we'll get going.' I say to Iskra. He seems relieved and nods.

'Of the blessing of god,' he imitates Mo and starts to laugh but I don't.

We head back. Iskra seems to feel better and talks about what we would do later after these adventures. I walk with him to Shabela's house and while he goes up the wooden stairs, I stop at the first step. My head is throbbing from the events of the day and I'm put off by the effort it would take to climb them. Enough has happened.

'Let's get going,' I say again.

I put the knife into a piece of folded rice paper and slide it straight into my back pocket. Even with the rain the heat has changed again to intense. The cooling that came with the changing of the tide has worn away. It hurts to stand motionless beneath the blinding sheets that pour down like yellow silver from the sky. Whether we stay or go makes no difference. Something vague sleeps within me that I struggle to understand; maybe it is the Dada telling me of all the ports he has visited, San Francisco, Montreal and Liverpool, a yearning somehow.

'The Malays love their power too much here,' the Dada says, 'the way they love their white Rajahs who rule for a hundred years without any trouble. It is within them to be dominated. The Chinese are an afterthought. The Sea Dayaks do not count at all. This is why they hate me so much.'

He laughs when the detectives come for him. To my mother he quietly says:

'Where is the support of my family in this game of chess?' She would go quiet and give no answer, her hands folded quietly her lap, but her look would be like death itself.

Time passes and my mood gets better. Sunday drifts into night. We laugh and smoke and sing to the moon.

Shabela comes down and we raise the pipe again and smoke at the edge of the sand till darkness falls upon us. We look at the stars across the water. They calm me but I am still strung between the notes laid down by the harmonica and the words of the lady in blue; as restless as the waves across last night's crumpled sheets. Something of them rise and fall inside me.

We say goodbye to Shabela and his wife. She says that she will invite the woman in blue again.

'She talks more than her prayers but she's a good friend,' she says.

'She knows you well,' she adds. I nod and feel that hollowness rise inside me again.

'You must bring these brave boys over some other time,' she says to Iskra.

'We don't get as many as interesting as you around here.'

Iskra laughs. We pay Shabela. Iskra laughs again and puts his arm around Mo. Shabela's wife swims in and out of my vision as she waves goodbye after us. The house is black against the water.

Shabela's rocks are as light as the silver paper they come wrapped in; safe as salt lightning in my pocket. He waves to us beneath the moon. Iskra seems happy. He sings as we drive all the way back to the city. We take a ride around the waterfront bars and decide which ones we want to return to later. We take a look in a café here, a soft drink there, gaze at brown bars where the women from Burma lie down in back rooms. It adds to our mood. We burn the amphetamine in a big bar with a karaoke room full of music and love flowing from every one of its aisles. The smells of jasmine where it has once been smoke rolls in on the breeze from Kalimantan and we suck deep and blow out solemnly. I should feel good but instead I am hot and cold at the same time in sudden uncertain spasms that have afflicted me since early morning. I remember the words of the Kalimantan nurse at Dada's funeral.

'In the end you catch a chill.'

I have eaten enough. We break the crystal there and then. It can leave you hungry. If you are empty to begin with it leaves you hollow, desolate. There is no point in losing the rush by searching for food. The music is within me now and makes me think of the markets and the mountains of fish that need to be distributed tomorrow, a mountain of silver, streaked with red waiting for me on the morning tide, a million dead eyes, no matter how warm the water or strong the sun.

We spend long hours in the bars and coffee houses talking and laughing then think about going back to the waterfront where we can stay all night without disturbance. We joke about the events of the day. Iskra said his honour is redeemed and suddenly I feel fine. It is all about honour.

We see the white boys trying to make it with the women. We ignore them. We are safe in our cocoon of the city. Fuck these Indos, always coming here causing trouble. They share our island but not our Sarawak home. Iskra takes the pipe out again and Mo does his party piece with the stick and turns the rice paper across his fingers like a grill. It provides a cushion for the holy rock that burns on its blanket of silver paper. What do tourists know of our lives? A rainbow falls across me, symmetry restored whose arc has been shattered by the day and let loose in tiny images from within my Dada's room.

We dance slowly by ourselves in open bars and closed ones across the waterfront. When they close we follow our path to the Chinese quarter that stays open all night. They obey their own laws here. I dance in the great hope and dreams of the pirates, an easy fortune, a swift life, sailing the waters that surround us and across all the islands of the Greater Sunda, our home as Sea Dayaks. We are not people of the jungle, the mountain or the plantation estates.

'Let me soothe you.' Mo says.

He is dancing. His arms rise in a slow rhythm until one hand hangs languidly above his head. He leans his body into a warrior pose that he doesn't keep but moves in the shape of a butterfly in slow movements across the floor. His hair flows down his white suit. He looks beautiful. He is beautiful.

The music rocks and shatters me at the same time. We blast high and then fall slowly down like a moon burst of sea snails in a trawl, inexorable as a clutch of silver stars cascading down onto the beach. A journey without fear opens out before me, without borders, without guards, without constraints on all who we are.

'I am a Sea Dayak.' I say.

Maybe it is why the white Rajahs control us for so long, because they are bland and pragmatic and we are a people lost within our own dreams of the great robbery, the furious work, the simplicity of the moment that only chance provides. Perhaps they know we cannot imagine ourselves as pirates forever. They would leave the Malays to deal with us. Dada is always the traitor when he decries the suburbs around Kuching, the ancient port of the Chinese and now the flower of western Borneo. It means nothing to him. The power of life no longer exists beyond the railings of his ships.

'If you go away your place is no longer in bondage to the State,' he used to say. He refuses the barriers that constrain my father.

The white boys continue arguing. They have followed us as surely as the Kalimantans in their flowered shirts who pursue us to the beach. Our peace is molested by their shouts and screams. The time we normally sit solemn as the night slides away is threatened just as the following mornings will find us at work when they are in their beds. It is hard, our silence transgressed, just as the young Burmese women are kept low in the bowels of the dirty Thai trawlers until the hour before the dawn when they bring them ashore to sell them.

The boy's shouts continue. They seem to be looking over at us without seeing as they crash between tables. Is this what they have come here for; their journey around our island, to drink and to shout at each other as if we do not exist? They regard us from dazed eyes that are red and look tired from their long journeys; as if they have worked long hours before the purchase of their tickets to paradise from Europe or Australia. They go straight to the bottle. Inside I feel calm but the dazzling explosions of the day, the stories of the lady in blue and the opaque mocking features of the Indonesians; their faces translucent amidst the rain and sea all weigh against me. Something drifts towards me like an ominous poison cloud.

'I'll deal with this,' Iskra says.

He stands up and staggers. His bandaged arm hangs by his side. I guide him back to his seat. I find myself gasping for breath as if I am under water. My heart sends little waves to wash over me. Rain dances on the matted roof. It would not last. The lemon light of the sun would come again tomorrow. Shabela's pipe passes between us. Iskra has taken it with him as an act of rage at his honour so cruelly ripped and not properly defended, no matter what he says. Shabela would not mind. He would say 'and of the blessings of god'. We laugh.

'Everything they touch is ripped from us,' Iskra says suddenly.

He grimaces in a tight smile as he smokes and makes a fist of his face. I can hear my Dada say:

'We all revolve around our own deceptions.'

Iskra's white shirt seems whiter and whiter, his skin darker along the forearms. Somewhere in the course of the day he has lost his gangster cap

The white boys are as restless as fireflies. They stand and then suddenly sit down; then rise again and roar with laughter, near to tears, like ferocious two-year-old twins. They put their hands up like make-believe fighters. They are intent upon creating uproar in the face of our silence. These sacred moments that come to the end of our day when our uneasy lives are swept clean and our drugs brought here on containers ships at Setubong with their constant supplies of Ya Bang.

I walk slowly towards the boys on deadened feet. My shoes are gone. I can feel my forehead swelling from the intense heat beating inside me, as if trying to force me back. Each time I feel its hot blast rise up against my face, I clench my teeth, tighten my fists in my pocket and, strain with all my being to engage with the dazzling fire of the lights above. My jaw tenses each time a piercing ray strobes me from the ceiling.

Dada is my father.

The woman in blue is my mother.

I am the baby passed over.

The roaring in my ears, a white seashell of a piece of coral breaks away inside me. I am one of those jig-saw puzzles of my childhood, each block slowly put together or taken away by my mother and father. I am walking on a glass carpet and my feet are bloody. It feels I walk for a long time on this shining roll. I can see the dark shape of my tiny baby steps like star fish in the phosphorus. In the distance the funnel of a tour-ist boat hoots away into the night, its lights hang like necklaces from the deck and hanging with them is the shape of my Dada's face as he turns away from me...

My own body is breaking up before me, surrounded by the blinding lights of the disco floor. I am helpless as a shipwreck in the dreams which woke me this morning. I think about the cool water and the Kalimantan fighters behind the rock. I want to return to the soft sound of the stream, to the sunlight at my Dada's funeral, to find peace once more in the shade, but the boys' faces are closer now and fierce. They raise their long white arms and their voices towards me. I want them quiet. I want everything to be quiet.

'We have our own ways here,' Iskra says, his voice comes like a sharp echo behind me.

I turn and see the eyes on my table before me, the eyes from every table in that place and then suddenly clear, the look from one of the white boys, his gaze as deep and disturbed as dark liquid. He peers at me as if from the bottom of the sea.

All I have to do is turn around and walk away. Blighted faces within the shadows press against me and push me forward. I take a few steps across the floor. The boys continue with their argument. Their bodies move and jerk like puppets brought from Java. They still seem quite far away although it could be my eyes. I can feel drops of sweat gathering above my eyebrows. It is the same relentless sun and pouring rain but this time inside me, bitter as cigarette smoke and black coffee as are all of Dada's absences.

Every vein throbs beneath my skin. I am being flayed. I cannot stand it but I take another step forward. I know it is stupid. I know I cannot shake off the whole of this day or all that I possess by simply putting one foot in front of another but it comes just the same, one single step forward and this time it is not a Kalimantan who stands before me but a tall white boy.

He opens his hand like a shovel. He balls his fingers into a fist and raises the threat towards me.

He raises the other and thrusts deep into what has been searching for me all this time.

His eyes follow my every movement. The sweat that has gathered on my eyebrows suddenly rushes down into my eyes, blinding me with a warm, heavy veil of salt and tears.

All I can feel are the club lights crashing like cymbals against my forehead. The silver ring on his first finger spins like a disco ball.

'What are you doing here May lay boy?' he cries.

The force of his words is like a crashing wave against my cheek. He rises from his chair, tall in his yellow tee shirt and strong, beautiful arms. Drunk, he laughs;

'This is no place for you,' he says.

'May-Lay.' He says it as if he owns the word and knows nothing of our lives here. He slaps my face. The force echoes deep within me like a wave on its own ignorant swell. The fabric of my being clings like a sail to my skin.

He steps forward and slaps me again. The blow shatters my physical world; a force that strikes everything from my existence. The floor sways beneath me.

'Is Tibet fucking Chinese?' he roars.

The dark club opens like a moonlit night at sea. It seems to heave with all my humiliation. From end to end it pours out its luminous opacity down upon me. My whole body tenses. The knife is there in my hand. I feel the metal come away from the smooth tissue of paper. I jerk the blade in his direction, the direction of the white boy. He stares at me wide eyed. It is with that first lunge that it begins. I shake off my sweat and realize that I have destroyed the natural balance of the world. The exceptional silence of the night where it has once dwelled within me is broken. The weapon jumps around as though with a life of its own. It seems to make little trace. All I hear is the sound of laughing and crying and then a sudden terrified scream.

'He's stabbed me. He's fucking stabbed me.'

I see the woman in blue. I hear again her gushing stories while she turns her earring between her fingers and burns me with her eyes. They are as wide as lamps.

'Do not judge all those born on the wrong side of the blanket,' she says.

My mother !!!!

Time after time, the weapon sinks itself into the fatal lines between destiny and history. One boy is laid before me, another by the door where he has tried to run towards the water. His clothes are torn. I am buried in a welter of arms and legs and the terrified, yet curious faces of the Malays, Dayaks and Chinese. I do what pirates always do, kill or be killed, nothing happens without a cause. Tables are overturned; there is a stampede of feet. Blood spatters Mo's white suit. It stains Iskra's bandage where he has tried to pull me away. The police are called. We are placed under arrest. They bundle us into a shining blue police van, its sides marked by the symbol of the flag. They take us to the station where all identities are forced or forged. We are accompanied by the sound of sirens. It notifies the world of our passage through the deep wet night. It announces the testimonies that would be told against me, a Sea Dayak of this island.

Available summer 2020

Seal of Secrets, our second book by Lin, translated from the original Chinese by the author, will be available this summer.

Can one piece of magic reveal a man's greatest fear? Can this magic make hundreds of people see their greatest fears at the same time? Can it transform people between evil and good?
In 2010, Li Meijia a young magician died during her show, which changed the destiny of Ge Yancheng, a rising literary star. He abandoned his ambition and his love and buried his name. In 2013, a mysterious letter opened his old wounds. Someone knew his secret.